Deadly Triangles

Margaret Tessler

Margaret Tessler

BookLocker.com, Inc.
2009

RECURRING CHARACTERS

<u>SALAZAR FAMILY</u>:
Sharon & Ryan Salazar live in San Antonio, often spend weekends in Port Aransas.
> Sharon is a lawyer;
> Ryan, a high-school English teacher.

Alana & Beto Meléndez—Ryan's sister & her husband, who live in Zapata, Texas
> Miguel Meléndez—their 19-year-old son,
> > law student at St. Mary's/San Antonio
> Gabe Meléndez—their 17-year-old son,
> > a high-school student
> Carlos Meléndez—their 10-year-old son,
> > a grade-school student

Leo Salazar—Ryan & Alana's brother
> a nurse at Santa Rita's in San Antonio
Ysela & Ricardo Salazar (Amá & Apá)—
> Ryan, Alana, & Leo's parents (live in Zapata)
Tío Roque—Apá's brother, friend of Mayra Montaño;
> owns the cottages where the Salazar/Meléndez
> families spend occasional weekends

"BIANCA" & HER FAMILY

Bertha Lumpkin/Bianca LaCroix/Bimbo—
     Miguel's love interest
Cordelia Lumpkin—Bianca's sister
John Addison—their uncle, manager of Villa Sonrisa,
     the mobile-home park next to Tío Roque's cottages

POLICE OFFICERS

Sgt. Bullis & Sgt. Fay—first to question Sharon & Ryan
Lt. Richmond—lead investigator

COFFEE-KLATCH NEIGHBORS

Mayra Montaño—flamboyant lady who hosts
     coffee klatches; friend of Tío Roque
Lydia Wilson—reminds Sharon of Raggedy Ann;
     married to Tom Wilson
Doris Hood (brusque, but good-hearted)
Thelma Bigelow (sourpuss)—married to Slim Bigelow
Ornella Hewett—(nondescript; mousy)
     married to Keith Hewett
Fina Borrego—married to Dan Borrego
Gloria Bullis—married to Sgt. Don Bullis

MANICURISTS

Marlene—married to Al
Helen—married to Roy

ACKNOWLEDGMENTS

It would be impossible to list everyone who helped make this book possible—either directly with practical suggestions or indirectly through their encouragement and faith in me.

However, I'll start by thanking retired peace officers Don Bullis and Damon Fay, as well as Lt. Darryl Johnson of the Port Aransas Police Department, for their invaluable help with my questions about police procedure. I'm also grateful to my daughter Mary Behm for her legal expertise and to my friend Pat Wood for her technical assistance. Whenever I stray from their collective wisdom, it's my own fault, not theirs. Sometimes (as they know) I simply like to color outside the lines.

Enormous gratitude goes to everyone who read my numerous drafts and provided useful feedback—Jerry Aguirre; my sister Lisa Gibson; my daughter Valerie Coffee; my comadre Merlinda Sedillo-Welch; my husband, Howard; and members of my writing workshops: Dave Bachelor, Mary Blanchard, Charlene Dietz, Edie Flaherty, Jeanne Knight, Betsy Lackmann, Marcia Landau, Jan McConaghy, Helen Pilz, Ronda Sofia, Pat Wood (again), and Mary Zerbe. Also thanks to Helen for providing the cover photo of Mustang Island.

A special thanks to Susanna Hackett Taylor. When I questioned my path, she inspired me to embrace my creative DNA. Without her, this book would still be in limbo.

Any mistakes are mine alone.

DEDICATION

For Wanda Crain, who cheers me up and cheers me on

Deadly Triangles

Chapter 1

I had tried to like Bimbo, which—when you stop to think about it—is the same as saying I never liked her. Was it because I didn't trust her? Doesn't matter now. Much as I disliked and distrusted her, I wouldn't have wished her dead. I especially wouldn't have wished her dead right there on our doorstep, so to speak.

But there we found her, stabbed to death, in our front yard. Well, not exactly *our* front yard. My husband, Ryan, and I were spending the weekend at Tío Roque's complex on Mustang Island along with other members of our family. Ryan's parents were staying in one of the cottages, his sister Alana and her family in another, and his brother Leo with us.

While out for a jog early Saturday morning, Leo discovered Bimbo's body on our lawn near the curb. He called nine-one-one on his cell phone, and within minutes two patrolmen arrived.

They cordoned off our whole front yard with yellow tape. So for the time being, Leo, Ryan, and I were confined to going in and out our back door. Meanwhile, all our neighbors and relatives—most of them wrapped in bathrobes and sporting tousled hair—tumbled out of their cottages like clowns out of tiny cars.

Other officers arrived and asked everyone a few basic questions. Then our family gravitated toward Ryan's parents' cottage while the police, EMTs, medical examiner, and various technical people finished their jobs.

My name is Sharon Salazar. Although I'm an attorney, most of the trouble I find myself in stems from my private life and not my law practice. This was the case with Bimbo.

After the initial horror of her grisly death, I began to puzzle over why we'd been dragged into her finale. If I sound flip it's because that's my way of dealing with anxiety. The truth is, not only was I sickened by her murder, I knew it was only a matter of time before the police would put the pieces together and probably come to the wrong conclusion.

Chapter 2

In the few minutes before the police arrived, I had caught only a glimpse of Bimbo's pale face, twisted in a mask of shock, and of her blood-smeared clothes. Before the scene could fully register, Leo placed his hands on my shoulders and forced me to turn away. But it was still hard to erase those few distorted moments from memory.

The next morning Ryan and I took a walk along the beach. Mustang Island—one in a string of barrier islands curving around the Texas coastline—has long been a magnet for us, and we were determined to fill our minds with nothing but the rhythm of the surf and the beauty surrounding us. Rose-colored morning glories hugged the dunes, nestled among sprawling dark green vines, while pale golden sea oats waved in the steady breeze.

"Feel better?" Ryan asked, gently squeezing my hand.

I nodded. "Much. After...after yesterday, I wasn't sure I wanted to come back here again."

"I know."

Ryan and I walked for several minutes before he spoke again. "This might sound callous...but...it seems that woman makes trouble even when she's dead."

I'd had the same thought, but hadn't acknowledged it till now. "You're thinking about Miguel, aren't you."

"Right. And us too."

"Us too," I echoed. "I don't want her death to run us off the Island."

Ryan put his arm around me and drew me closer. "That's the one thing we don't have to worry about."

*   *   *

That afternoon two detectives from the Port Aransas Police Department arrived to "ask some routine questions."

I rarely think of myself as getting older, but as I near forty, I find people often look way too young for their professions. I guessed—wrongly I'm sure—Sgt. Fay to be about seventeen. His partner, Sgt. Bullis, appeared only slightly older—twenty at best. Both were of medium height and build; one was blond, the other brunet. The Hardy Boys meet Nancy Drew. Only I felt more like Miss Marple than Nancy right now.

Sgt. Fay declined our offer of iced tea, but Sgt. Bullis accepted and followed Ryan into the kitchen.

"Tell me, Ms. Salazar," Sgt. Fay asked politely, after he was seated on the beachwood sofa in our living room, "how well did you know Bertha Lumpkin?"

"Who?"

His face was impassive. "Bertha Lumpkin. The dead woman. When did you first meet her?"

"Oh. I always thought of her as—something else—I mean—" I paused to collect myself. "Sorry to seem so dense. It's just that I never knew her by that name. She'd told us it was Bianca LaCroix."

He nodded, and I caught a twinkle in his blue eyes before he returned to his no-nonsense demeanor.

I gave him the bare-bones version of my initial meeting with Bertha/Bianca/Bimbo, figuring he wouldn't be interested in hearing about the colorful Japanese lanterns Mayra Montaño had strung around her yard the night of her patio party or the bowls of peach-colored bougainvillea that adorned the tables.

"I first met—uh, Bertha—at a neighborhood get-together a couple of months ago. Right around Labor Day, I think. I don't recall that we had any conversation, beyond maybe 'hi'—you know, the usual greetings." I clasped my hands together to keep from crossing my fingers. I wondered if Ryan was answering the same question and if our stories would match.

"And later? After you learned she was involved with your nephew?" Sgt. Fay asked. "You had occasion to talk with her then?"

My heart sank on hearing that she'd already been linked with Miguel. Hiding my dismay and ignoring the hint of sarcasm I heard in his voice, I smiled sweetly and veered away from his question. "She had a number of admirers. But I'm sure you already know that."

In turn, he ignored my remark. "When did you last see Ms. Lumpkin?"

"It's been awhile." Seeing his expression, I added, "I don't mean to sound vague. But it was a few weeks ago, and I really didn't give it any thought at the time."

"Where was this?"

"Walking along the beach. From a distance. I'm not sure she even saw me."

"She was alone?"

"No."

"With your nephew?"

"Yes."

"When did you see him last?"

For a moment I couldn't even remember what day it was. "Day before yesterday, I think. Friday. We got here that afternoon."

"Was he with Ms. Lumpkin then?"

"No." My head started hurting and I felt like screaming, *How could he be with her then if I hadn't seen her in weeks?*

I reminded myself he was just doing his job, took a deep breath, and continued calmly. "We were at his parents' place—Ryan's sister's place. Miguel stopped in to say hello and left again shortly after that." I could see the question coming. "He didn't say where he was going."

Sgt. Fay took another tack. "We know Ms. Lumpkin was killed sometime before six-thirty yesterday morning. Can you tell me if you saw or heard anything unusual, say from nine-o'clock the night before up till then?"

We'd been asked that right after she was found, but were too much in shock to think clearly. I wrapped my arms around myself, the image of her lifeless body jolting me again.

"Do you remember anything you might not have thought of at the time?" he continued.

I searched my memory for a few moments, then nodded. "The people next door have a little dog—Yorkie-mix, I think. It sleeps on their screened porch. Ryan and I both heard it barking in the middle of the night."

"Did you check to see why it was barking?"

"Ryan thought it just wanted to go inside. But I thought it sounded—agitated. I looked out the kitchen window, into their back yard. Of course, I didn't see anything there. A minute or two later, I heard a car drive by and figured that was what was bothering Barky."

"Did you check on the car?"

"Kind of. It was nearly out of sight by the time I got to the front window. I just caught a glimpse of taillights. Nothing else."

Sgt. Fay raised a skeptical eyebrow. "You didn't see Ms. Lumpkin out front? Didn't hear any other noise?"

"No. If she cried out or called for help, I hate to think I didn't hear her." Something Leo said that I'd blocked out now stirred at the edge of my mind. "She must have already been unconscious—or dead." My imagination filled in the blanks. I hadn't heard the sound of car doors opening and closing, hadn't heard Bianca's body being dumped out, if that's what had happened. My distress was genuine. "How awful!"

His voice softened. "Do you know what time it was?"

"That I do. I looked at the clock because I wondered if I should go back to sleep or if it was almost time to get up. Anyway, it was three-twenty, and I went back to bed."

Before Sgt. Fay could question me further, Sgt. Bullis and Ryan returned to the living room. "I wish I could have been more helpful," Ryan said as they seated themselves.

The tension eased from my shoulders. I hoped Ryan's comment meant that he'd been as noncommittal (while trying to look cooperative) as I'd tried to be.

"We only come up here on weekends now and then," he continued. "I'm afraid we don't know any of the residents too well."

"But well enough that Mrs. Montaño invited you to a party?" Sgt. Fay directed the question at me. Young, he might be, but not dumb.

"That was so we could get acquainted. Now we know people to wave to and say hello." I smiled. "There's a friendly atmosphere in the neighborhood, but that's about it. Not really a lot of socializing otherwise."

Sgt. Fay looked down at his notes, probably to keep from commenting on how unneighborly it was for someone to murder Bianca.

"Your brother is the one who found Ms. Lumpkin?" Sgt. Bullis asked Ryan.

"Yes."

"Is he here now? We'd like to talk to him again too."

"He went back to San Antonio yesterday afternoon. Had to go to work today—he's a nurse at Santa Rita's." Ryan didn't add that the first thing on Leo's agenda was to talk to Miguel. "Sharon and I have a couple of extra days off. Fall break. We're planning to go home Tuesday."

The two officers exchanged glances.

"When will you be back?" Sgt. Bullis asked.

"Couple of weeks if the weather's good," Ryan answered.

None of us needed to be reminded it was still hurricane season. But at this point, a hurricane seemed more welcome than the investigation ahead.

"Any idea why this happened at your place?" Sgt. Fay asked.

I shook my head. "The only thing I can think of, Tío Roque might have rented it out when we weren't here. Maybe the killer thought someone else was staying here."

"Or maybe, like I told Sgt. Bullis, he got the cottages confused," Ryan added. "There're ten altogether. And they all look somewhat alike from the outside."

"We already got the list of tenants from your uncle," Sgt. Fay said. "No connection to Ms. Lumpkin—except of course in *your* family. Nothing on the surface anyway, but we'll keep digging."

"Good. I'm sure something else will turn up," I said pointedly.

"We'll keep in touch," Sgt. Bullis said, as the officers stood to leave.

I bet you will. We'd given our home and work addresses plus our various telephone numbers to the investigating officers when they questioned us yesterday, and I could almost feel our leash shrinking.

Chapter 3

The term "trailer park" sometimes conjures an image of rickety trailers in unkempt yards dotted by rusting pickups. In stark contrast, *Vista Sonrisa* was a community of forty upscale, stylishly designed mobile homes—each on a large lot—with well-kept gardens and late-model cars kept discreetly under their respective carports.

(The owner of the mobile-home park thought "*sonrisa*" meant sunrise, but "Smiley View" has a friendly sound just the same.)

Tío Roque's ten cottages, adjacent to the park, were equally attractive, with brand-new wood siding stained a weathered gray. Palm trees lined the semi-circular street, and oleander hedges, dappled in pink, white, and green, separated each front yard.

A picket fence edged the property in back—otherwise, there weren't any fences separating the back yards from one another, their boundaries marked only by individual lawns or gardens. A footpath ran behind the picket fence and eventually connected with the mobile-home park. Beyond the path were the sand dunes; beyond the dunes, the beach.

Mayra Montaño's double-wide on a corner lot in Vista Sonrisa was the ideal setting for a large party. And Mayra's innate curiosity made her privy to all the neighborhood gossip.

Mayra herself was a rather flamboyant character whose fashion sense followed her idiosyncrasy du jour. The night of her get-acquainted luau she'd worn a flowing muumuu patterned in plate-sized red hibiscus. Her too-black hair was pulled into a bun on top of her head, with sticks poking out. I think it was supposed to look Japanese.

It was hard to believe her party had taken place nearly two months ago—seven weeks to be exact. It was there that we first met Bianca. So much had happened in the meantime, it seemed more like seven months. I suspect the only reason our family was invited is that Mayra, a widow in her late sixties, had her eye on Tío Roque, a confirmed bachelor, also in his sixties.

Still, the evening was balmy and the crowd congenial, so we were glad to be included. In addition to the festive decorations, Hawaiian music floated through the air. Soon after we'd arrived and greeted other guests, Ryan, Leo, and I wandered over to a softly bubbling fountain, where we sipped mai tais and sampled hors d'oeuvres.

As we chatted together, a cutesy airhead in hot-pink short-shorts and a spaghetti-strapped tee sidled up to Ryan. She placed her fuchsia-nailed fingertips on his arm, gently, so as not to jostle his drink. I wondered if I should suggest that the coy effect was muddied when she batted her eyes so energetically. Then again, maybe one of her contacts had simply wandered off and she was trying to maneuver it back in place.

Her eyes were a startling shade of blue, her hair bottle blonde. (A natural blonde myself, I can always spot these things.) Otherwise she was fairly attractive. She had a small, pixy-shaped face with cupid-bow lips, which lent her a deceptive air of innocence.

"So you're Miguel's Uncle Ryan," she cooed. "You're just as handsome as he is—those deep brown eyes and that thick black hair. I could have taken you for twins!"

Rule Number One: Never flirt with a man whose wife is standing right beside him.

"I've heard so much about you," she babbled on.

To Ryan's credit, he moved back a small step. "All good, I hope."

She giggled. "Well, of course."

"Actually, I'm Ryan's twin," Leo said.

Fraternal twins, Ryan and Leo bore a facial resemblance, but differed in build, Leo being the heftier of the two. Ironically, Miguel did resemble Ryan more than Leo did.

She turned toward Leo, as if suddenly noticing other people present. Her eyelids quit twitching, or whatever they were doing. "Oh. Well. Hmm. Yes. I see the likeness."

"And you are—" I asked, keeping my voice cool and my smile fake. The only clue to my irritation was the way I kept twirling the little paper umbrella from my drink.

"Oh, excuse me. Where are my manners? I'm Bianca LaCroix."

"And this is my wife, Sharon," Ryan said, linking the fingers of his free hand with mine, the little umbrella crumpled between them.

"So you're a friend of Miguel?" Leo asked.

"I suppose you could call us 'friends.'" She gave us a sly look as her fingers made imaginary quotation marks.

Leo scanned the crowd. "Where is Miguel?"

"He had to do something with 'mommy and daddy.'" She made air quotes again, her tinkly laugh not quite hiding her annoyance. "I guess that's what happens when you're dating a younger guy."

I blinked. How old was this bimbo anyway? Looking more closely at the tiny lines around her eyes, I guessed she was nearer my age than Miguel's nineteen years.

"I thought...."

Ryan squeezed my hand hard, which I correctly interpreted as a signal to be quiet.

"Well, look who's here!" Leo said, motioning one of Mayra's elderly neighbors to join us. "Mr. Edwards, good to see you!"

Mr. Edwards tottered toward us on spindly legs sticking out from brown Bermuda shorts. He peered at us through thick trifocals, his gaze finally resting on Bianca. "There you are, my dear—looking cute as a button," he cackled.

Her eyes glazed over as she drifted away with a languid wave. "You too," she told Mr. Edwards over her shoulder, leaving me to ponder the cuteness of buttons.

Mr. Edwards excused himself to trail unsteadily in her wake.

"I thought Alana and Beto would be here too," I said, finishing my interrupted thought.

"So did I," Leo answered. "Maybe they'll drop in later."

"With Miguel in tow?" Ryan shook his head. "Maybe 'mommy and daddy' really did come up with some plan to avoid what's-her-name."

"If she really is 'dating' Miguel"—Leo made exaggerated air quotes—"then Alana must be having fits."

"Miguel is smart, funny, good-looking," I said. "He could go out with any number of girls. Why...Bimbo?"

Leo & Ryan exchanged glances.

"Guys his age don't always think with their brains," Leo explained.

"Never mind. No graphics, please."

Using her cane, another of Mayra's neighbors inched her way over to us, then shook her bony finger under Ryan's nose. "Young man, I hope you weren't taken in by that hussy!"

Ryan's eyes twinkled. "Not at all."

I immediately warmed to her. "Mrs. Parker," I said, "How nice to see you again!"

"Again? Have we met?"

Oops, she must have forgotten that Mayra introduced us earlier, so I re-introduced myself.

She glared at me. "I know who you are. You don't have to tell me over and over. Do you think I'm a dingbat?"

"I'm sorry. We've met so many people, I'm not always sure who, when, or where. Have you already met Ryan and Leo?"

Once we'd established that Ryan was my husband and Leo my brother-in-law, she began another tirade.

"Young man, you have a beautiful wife. Why are you taking up with that vixen? I saw you two going into the Snowy Egret yesterday, arm-in-arm, and I know what that means."

We were all startled speechless for a few moments. The Snowy Egret Inn boasted a lavish buffet in addition to its rooms. Maybe Miguel and Bianca had gone there for lunch, or afternoon tea. Or afternoon something.

"You have me confused with someone else," Ryan told Mrs. Parker, stone-faced. "I have a relative who looks a lot like me."

"Well, why didn't you say so?" she demanded crossly.

Mr. Edwards suddenly reappeared, having apparently been unable to catch up with Bianca. "There you are, my dear," he addressed Mrs. Parker. "I've been looking all over for you!"

"Men!" Mrs. Parker swiped her cane in Mr. Edward's direction, then hobbled away. Mr. Edwards, undeterred, shuffled after her.

"I need to have a talk with my nephew," Ryan muttered.

No more "boys will be boys"? I wondered what Ryan could say that Alana and Beto hadn't already said. But then, Miguel had always looked up to his uncles, so maybe a word from them would sink in…. And maybe not.

Chapter 4

"I suppose I should be flattered," Ryan remarked as we got ready for bed, "that Mrs. Parker mistook me for someone twenty years younger."

"I started to say her eyesight must be failing," I teased. "But she called me beautiful, so it must be twenty-twenty after all."

Ryan laughed. "At least she was right about that."

I stood in the doorway between the bedroom and bathroom, massaging face cream into my skin. Ryan was sitting on the edge of the bed, skimming through a travel brochure on Las Vegas, New Mexico.

"Now that I've had a little time to think about it—and don't need to scratch her eyes out anymore—I don't understand why Bianca was so cold to Leo. He doesn't look as much like Miguel as you do, but there's still a family resemblance. Why didn't she latch onto him too?"

"I don't know." Ryan put the brochure down and stared off into space. "Maybe she knows Leo's gay."

"Well, she knows you're married, and that didn't stop her."

"Yeah, it was a little much. I figured she was just trying—in her own clueless way—to get in good with Miguel's family."

"Which includes Leo *and* me.

"And about two-hundred other people she doesn't know yet."

"And another thing—"

"Honey, you're thinking like a lawyer. Forget Bianca. Miguel will see the error of his ways, and we'll never see her again."

If only that had proved to be true.

* * *

Miguel surprised me by calling me at my office the following week and asking me to meet him for lunch. We'd all gone home after the long Labor Day weekend and (I supposed) gotten back into our respective routines. Miguel was studying pre-law at St. Mary's University, so lived in San Antonio in a small apartment off campus. (The rest of his family—the Meléndezes—lived in Zapata, a town 200 miles farther south, as did the Salazar parents.)

I worked in the Pan American building, a few short blocks from the Riverwalk, and arrived at Tony Roma's only minutes before Miguel. We exchanged hugs, then sat down to order our sandwiches. Throughout the meal, we stuck to small talk.

We exhausted the topics of school and work and polished off our barbecue & coleslaw. I knew Miguel had something else on his mind, but wasn't quite prepared for the abrupt way he brought it up.

"Sharon, will you talk some sense into my mom?"

My eyes widened. "Excuse me?"

"She'd listen to you. Maybe she'd quit doing that matchmaking sh— stuff."

The waiter picked that time to appear with our check and tell us he'd be our cashier but not to hurry. I looked around the busy restaurant and noticed people waiting.

"Let's walk over to the Alamo," I suggested. "We can find a quiet corner to sit and talk."

The bloody battles fought at the Alamo were at odds with the tranquility that now surrounded the mission. The courtyards were spacious and shady, my favorite refuge when I needed a peaceful place to think. Miguel and I found a bench under an ancient live oak where we could continue our conversation.

"You know why we missed Mrs. Montaño's party?" he grumbled. "My mom dragged me off to see an old college friend and her dorky daughter. Not too subtle."

"But that's not the real problem, is it."

He looked down at his hands, then back up at me. "Mom won't even try to get to know Bianca."

"I see. How serious is it with you two?"

"I like her a lot." He flushed. "Okay, more than a lot."

"Tell me about her. What makes her so special?"

His eyes narrowed as he searched my face for a trace of cynicism. I placed my hand on his arm.

"Miguel, I'm not being patronizing. I really want to know."

"I don't know where to start." He paused. "She's...well...she's sophisticated."

Not a word I would have chosen. I glanced away so my non-poker-face wouldn't betray me, but Miguel was studying a piece of grass he twisted between his fingers.

"She's been all over Europe. Germany, Italy, Monte Carlo, the French Riviera. She speaks three foreign languages."

"That *is* impressive! What brought her to Port Aransas?"

He shrugged. "Her uncle manages the mobile-home place, and he asked her to come down and help out. She's a salesperson or something."

"So that's how you met?"

"Yeah. This summer when the rest of you were on vacation. Gabe and I used to come to the Island on weekends."

"Well, you haven't known each other very long. Maybe it makes your mother nervous to see you so serious so quickly."

"I'm not going to do something stupid. She keeps reminding me I have six more years of school. Like I'd forgotten it."

I didn't say anything, and after a few moments, he grinned sheepishly. "I guess I sound kinda defensive, don't I."

"A little." I smiled at him.

"I know Mom means well, but sometimes...."

"What does your dad say?"

Miguel looked away. "Oh, the usual. Responsibility. Respect."

And practical matters like condoms, no doubt.

"Tell you what. I'll do this much. I'll try to get your mom to call off blind dates and dorky daughters."

He laughed. "Thanks. Now if she'd just try to like Bianca."

"That's fair enough. Bianca deserves a try."

* * *

Trying was trying, if you'll excuse the pun. Miguel now considered me an ally, and invited Ryan and me to go with them to an outdoor concert on the beach the next time we came to Mustang Island. I wasn't enthralled at the idea of spending any time with Bianca, but gritted my teeth and promised myself to be on my best behavior.

Friday evening the four of us met at the merry-go-round on Green Heron Beach with all our "luggage," as Ryan called it—beach chairs and a cooler filled with soft drinks. From there we dragged our stuff closer to the bandstand and found a place to set everything up.

We got situated just as the concert began. The band was *Scaly and the Lepers*, their style screechy and jerky. Bianca squealed in delight over each number. I smiled glassy-eyed and longed for a pair of earplugs. Another sign my age was telling on me.

At that point, I decided getting older had its advantages. I was kind of surprised Miguel hadn't outgrown the likes of Scaly too, but maybe the concert choice was another of Bianca's misguided attempts to recapture her youth.

Between numbers, we made a stab at conversation.

"I've always wanted to go to Italy, Bianca," I ventured. "Especially Venice. Which city was your favorite?"

She gave me a blank look. "Uh. Rome."

Good answer. I've heard of that one too.

"What did you think of the Coliseum?" Ryan asked.

"Well, you know how it is when you're on a tour. We were so rushed."

She turned her attention to Miguel, cupped her hand over his ear, and whispered something. They both giggled, but I heard him whisper, "Not now."

During the next intervals, she occupied herself with her cell phone. (First I knew there was such a thing as heavy-metal ringtones.)

The concert was mercifully short, possibly because it was free. Ryan and Miguel hauled the cooler back to Miguel's Jeep, while Bianca and I folded the chairs. As we walked to the parking lot, she jabbered about getting her nails done, and I responded with a series of "ums."

"But I'll never go to Marlene again," she stated.

"Um."

"She jabbed me with the nail scissors and pretended it was an accident."

"Um."

"It's not my fault her husband—well, never mind."

I surfaced from my lethargy enough to feel a mix of curiosity and sympathy regarding Marlene. About then we reached our cars and got busy with goodbyes.

"Let's do this again!" Bianca suggested. "They have these concerts all through September."

Ryan and I smiled and mumbled in unison.

"Good! It's a date."

I never had a chance to find out what we'd agreed to.

Chapter 5

Looking back now, I wonder if we could have done anything differently. Probably not, though a sliver of doubt haunts me from time to time.

I did have my pep talk with Alana the morning after the concert while we walked along the beach and picked up seashells. She mentioned that the matchmaking plots weren't working, which saved me the trouble of bringing it up.

"Alana, why don't you try a little reverse psychology instead?"

"He'd see right through that...too."

"Maybe so, but it wouldn't hurt. You could tell him that after talking with me, you realized you hadn't been very open. Something kinda vague. Tell him you'd like to invite Bianca for dinner. Say it'll be small—just the family."

Alana laughed. "*Just* the family? That's small?"

I laughed with her. "You can reassure him that it's just us 'weekenders' and not all two-hundred relatives."

Alana stooped to pick up an angel wing. She brushed the sand off, then stuck the shell in the pocket of her denim shorts. "Then what?"

We started walking again.

"Well, one of two things. Either Bianca will turn out to be the darling Miguel thinks she is, and we can all admit we were wrong. *Or* the reverse will happen and he'll see her through *our* eyes.

"Ha. I think he's wearing blinders."

"I do too," I admitted. "Still, I think when they're forced to interact with other people instead of staying wrapped up in their private cocoon, even Miguel can't help seeing what she's really like."

"Sounds dicey. Surely she can *act* pleasant through one meal."

"Maybe it'll take more than one. But it is fair. The only one who can make Bianca look bad is Bianca herself."

*   *   *

Alana didn't waste any time. She planned a dinner for the following Saturday and persuaded everyone to come back to the Island then. It was rare for any of us to come here two weekends in a row. Ryan and I—with our every-other-weekend routine—probably came the most often.

No one else had a set schedule. Alana and Beto's younger boys—Gabe, age seventeen, and Carlos, age ten—were often involved in school activities, which determined their comings and goings. The Salazar parents—Amá and Apá—came at random too. Sometimes Leo and his partner, Jeff, spent the weekend with their respective families, sometimes together. So it was quite a feat to get us all together at the same time.

"We need to take advantage of the nice weather while we can," Alana told us.

In truth, I think she was just anxious to get the dinner over with. When the big night arrived, I'm sure we all felt some level of anxiety. We had dressed casually, in tees, tank tops, or polos, with shorts or jeans. Bimbo's fluorescent green shorts were ultra short and her tube top ultra narrow. Carlos stared openly. The rest of us pretended not to notice and greeted her with as much enthusiasm as we could muster.

For Miguel's sake, I'd been making a serious attempt to think of her as Bianca instead of Bimbo, but some situations set me up for failure.

Miguel thunked Carlos on the head and whispered something to him. Carlos looked away, but stole a glance at her whenever Miguel wasn't looking. I think Carlos' honest reaction registered with Miguel, because he mumbled something about the evening getting cool and would she like a jacket. Since goosebumps were popping out on every inch of her overexposed skin, she agreed. Alana lent her a sweater.

Amá's lips were set in a prim line, so I winked at her, a silent reminder that we'd made a pact not to say or do anything to put Miguel on the defensive.

We moved to the patio, which stretched across the back of the cottage, and seated ourselves on white wicker furniture with plump sea-green cushions. We sat in a rather uneven semi-circle where we could look out at the small garden, neatly arranged with a variety of richly colored hibiscus. Miguel and Bianca were glued together in the middle of the arc, while the rest of us fanned out on either side.

We were munching on veggies and Fiesta Dip when Carlos' tiger-striped cat, Spot, sprang through the pet door onto the patio.

Bianca clasped her hand over her heart. "Oh, goodness. I hope he hasn't picked up any sand fleas!" she remarked in a breathy voice. Faux demure.

Spot looked at her with that stare cats have perfected, as if to say he hoped the same about her. Sometimes cats will seek out the one person in a crowd who doesn't seem to like them. Not so with Spot. He slunk under the glider where

Beto and Carlos were sitting and continued glowering at Bianca.

Carlos' face reddened, but just as he opened his mouth to defend his maligned pet, Beto, always kind and always a genial host, laid his hand on his son's shoulder and spoke in his soothing way.

"That could be a worry." Beto's gray eyes were gentle behind his rimless glasses. "But we keep a close eye on him, and we'd know if he had fleas."

"He stays in the house?"

"Yes, we don't want him to be a nuisance to the neighbors."

"Is he allowed in the kitchen?" Bianca smiled, but there was an edge to her voice.

Miguel spoke up. "Bianca found cat hair in her food at a fancy restaurant, and it really freaked her out."

"I should think so," Alana said.

Leo folded his hands behind his head and gazed out at the garden. "You don't need to worry about that here. Whenever Spot darkens the kitchen door, Alana chases him out with Lysol Spray."

"She follows all of us around with Lysol Spray," Gabe put in with a mischievous gleam in his eyes.

Alana laughed. "I'm not *that* bad."

"You're lucky we don't have a horse in here," Gabe added. "Carlos would adopt every animal he could if Mom and Dad would let him. They even had to make him quit watching *Animal Planet* all day long."

"I'm going to be a vet'rinarian when I grow up," Carlos said.

"Well, of course I like animals too," Bianca murmured, flashing an artificial smile.

Spot scowled, then emerged from under the glider and ambled toward her as if he'd like to hack up a hairball right on her flower-painted toenails.

I wondered if Amá had the same impression.

"I have an idea," she said. "Let's take Spot next door to our place, Carlitos." She bent down and beckoned Spot. He turned toward her out-stretched hands and allowed her to pick him up, then began purring softly.

Amá and Spot went through the garden, while Apá and Carlos retrieved Spot's food, water, and litter box from the utility room and carried them out the front door—out of Bianca's delicate sight.

I also wondered if Miguel was really that oblivious.

Chapter 6

By the time Spot's escorts returned, dinner was ready. Amá and I helped Alana bring dishes to the table while everyone else moved into the dining area. The dining table was round, lending itself to both comfort and conversation. The bright blue tablecloth was a good backdrop for the colorful dinnerware with its Aztec designs.

Meals were served family style, and I noticed that Bianca took very small portions of the various dishes, if any at all.

"I've heard that Mexican pottery contains a lot of lead," she said in her whispery way.

"That's probably true of some pottery," Alana replied with a smile. "But these are porcelain dishes I got at Target. They're perfectly safe."

"I can't eat fried foods," Bianca said, picking at her tamale.

"Actually, tamales are steamed."

"Whatever. Is it very spicy? I can't eat stuff that's too spicy."

Despite her good intentions, Alana couldn't help glaring at Miguel. "I wish you'd said something, Miguel. I'd have planned something else."

"Oh, that's okay," Bianca said. "I wouldn't want to put you to any trouble."

Once again, Beto intervened, steering the conversation away from food. "Bianca, my son tells me you're quite a linguist."

A perplexed frown clouded her face.

"What's a linguist?" Carlos asked.

Gabe grinned. "Someone who worships the god Linguini."

Bianca looked relieved, and I half-expected her to tell us she was actually a Presbyterian.

Beto laughed, explaining that Gabe considered himself a comedian, then answered Carlos. "It means she knows a lot of languages, mijo."

"Not too many," she said hastily.

Her cell phone jangled from the depths of her purse, which she'd left in the living room. She hurried to retrieve it, and—since both living and dining areas were open and since she fairly screamed, "Bitch!"—we couldn't help but hear.

"Thank goodness for caller ID," she remarked as she returned to the table. "I told that woman not to call me again." She rolled her eyes, but not before we saw the anger in them. "Some people!"

* * *

The meal dragged on without further incident. Afterwards, Amá and Apá made excuses to leave. Miguel took that as a cue for his own escape with Bianca. Alana and I finished putting food away and loading the dishwasher while the others watched ESPN.

Neither of us spoke much. Finally Alana said, "I guess I should be elated. But I'm not. I hadn't stopped to think how this would embarrass Miguel. Did you see his face? Especially after that phone call...the one she wouldn't answer."

"I know. Maybe it's small comfort," I said, "but none of us did anything to make her act the way she did."

"Except have the audacity to own a flealess cat. Oh, yes, and serve Mexican food."

"Maybe she really was scared of the dinnerware."

We both started giggling.

"I wonder what that call was all about," Alana said.

"A jealous wife, I bet."

Alana's shoulders slumped. "One way or another, Miguel is going to be hurt. How easy it was when he was little and I could kiss away his boo-boos. I don't have that magic anymore."

I put my arms around her, not knowing what to say, and she clung to me, weeping quietly.

Chapter 7

Later that night, all proverbial hell broke loose. I didn't learn about it till the next morning when the ringing of the phone jarred me from sleep. Ryan stirred, but didn't wake up. I reached across him to retrieve the phone from the nightstand.

The caller was Mayra Montaño.

"Did you hear about all the commotion?" she asked.

"What commotion?" I looked at the clock. Six a.m. What on earth caused Mayra to call so early?

"At Miss Hot-Pants' place."

"Who?"

"Miss Bianca La Croix, that's who. She lives two doors down from me. I almost called the police."

Suddenly wide awake, I felt my heart leap to my throat. "What happened?" *Where was Miguel?*

"When she came home with that nice young man—"

"My nephew?"

"Yes. He's the one. It wasn't that late. Maybe nine o'clock."

"Go on."

"Well!" Mayra paused, obviously relishing the suspense. "Thelma Bigelow was there waiting for her."

I'd met Thelma Bigelow at Mayra's luau three weeks ago. Mayra had beamed as she'd introduced us; Thelma's gray eyes had flicked over us without interest. As for me, I'd had to force myself not to stare at her red wig with its brassy highlights or her orangey-tan makeup that didn't hide the wrinkles in her face.

"Thelma was there. And then what?" I asked, prompting Mayra to take up her tale.

"She began screaming at Miss Hot-Pants. Then, before you know it, they were at each other's throats. Thelma kept yelling for Bianca to stay away from her husband."

I wondered if Thelma was last night's unknown caller. I wouldn't have suspected her of having a husband young enough to interest Bianca.

"How old are the Bigelows anyway?"

"She's sixty, one side or the other, with sun-damaged skin and—well, no matter. Slim is ten years younger. Might not have been much of a problem fifteen or twenty years ago. Hard to tell. He's a sanctimonious prig on the outside, but a letch inside. Thelma thinks he's a prize, which is the attraction for Miss Hot Pants. She sure likes to stir up trouble."

So it would seem. "Okay, I'm sorry I interrupted. Go on with what you were telling me." *Where does Miguel fit in all this?*

"Well, *then*—" Mayra paused again. I could imagine the sticks in her hair fairly quivering with anticipation.

"Yes?"

"Your nephew tried to get between Bianca and Thelma— to break it up, you know. So they started screeching and clawing at *him*."

I closed my eyes and took a deep breath to ease the tightness in my chest.

"Like I said, I was just about to call the police, but as suddenly as it started, it stopped. Bianca ran into her house and slammed the door, and your nephew and Thelma went their separate ways."

"I see. You must have some reason for telling me this." *At six in the morning.*

"It's something I thought you'd want to know." Mayra sounded miffed.

"You're right. And I thank you for not calling the police. I'll get in touch with Miguel and make sure everything's okay."

"Let me know."

"You bet."

After ending the call, I put on my comfy terrycloth robe and went into the kitchen to make coffee. Leo, in tee-shirt and cutoffs, got there about the same time.

"What's up?" he asked. "Who was calling so early?"

Glad for his company, I poured out the whole story, somehow forgetting to start the coffee. "I can't see any point in waking up everyone else. At the same time, I'm worried."

"So am I. I'm going to check on Miguel."

"I'm going with you."

"Then hurry up!"

I popped a breath mint—my tribute to oral hygiene—ran my fingers through my hair, and changed into a denim shorts set.

Leo and I walked three cottages over and counted cars. Alana and Beto's van was in the carport, Miguel's Jeep behind it. I started to go back to our cottage, but Leo stopped me with a hand on my arm. The overhead light had come on in the van.

"Stay here," he said, then walked over and opened the passenger door. A minute later he returned, propping up Miguel, who had scratches on his face as well as a black eye.

"Let's take him home and sober him up," Leo said.

By the time we got back, Ryan was up and wondering where we'd gone.

"I'll explain later," I mouthed as I started the forgotten coffee.

Miguel sat on the sofa while I dabbed at the scratches, relieved to see they weren't deep. Leo plied him with yerba buena, then sent him off to take a cold shower. While the water was running, Leo and I filled Ryan in on the morning's events.

When Miguel rejoined us, he was wearing a plaid bathrobe of Leo's that was several sizes too large. I collected his discarded clothes and threw them into the washer.

"I could've done that," he said.

"No problem. You just take it easy. Anything you want to talk about?"

"No."

"Okay. Are your folks expecting you to be home?"

"Oh, jeez. I'd better call 'em. I'm telling 'em you invited me for breakfast."

Of course Alana sensed something wrong and asked him to put me on the line.

"Did you invite Miguel and Bianca for breakfast?" She sounded accusing, as if I were collaborating with the lovebirds.

"No, I didn't ask Bianca. Leo—um—ran into Miguel this morning, and he looked like he needed cheering up."

Alana sighed. "Oh dear. Well, I guess he'll tell us in his own time."

"I'm sure he will."

* * *

Leo, Ryan, and I ate breakfast and read the Sunday paper while Miguel lay on the sofa and stared at the ceiling.

"Everyone will be dancing in the streets when they find out I'm not seeing Bianca anymore," he said glumly, breaking the silence.

"No one is gloating, Miguel," I told him. "No one wants to see you unhappy."

He closed his eyes and didn't speak again for several minutes. Then he murmured, "*She* makes people unhappy. She made some woman think she was fooling around with her husband. I don't think she was. Well, maybe she was. I don't know. But that woman felt miserable, and Bianca enjoyed seeing her that way."

"Are you sure?"

"Don't you believe me?"

"Of course I do. I just didn't expect your feelings about Bianca to change so radically. And so suddenly."

"Not that sudden."

He was quiet a while longer. "You know what started me thinking?" he said at last. "We argued about it on the way to her place."

I waited, not saying anything. But it wasn't her phoniness or even his own embarrassment that concerned him.

"She was rude to my mom," he said.

Tears pricked my eyes as a weight lifted from my heart.

"I'm going to get ready for Mass," I told the guys. "When I get back, it'll probably be time to start back for San Antonio."

"Wait up. I'll go with you," Ryan said.

"Light about a hundred candles for me," Miguel said.

I bent down and gave him an auntly kiss. "Always."

I'd like to say we lived happily ever after, but our troubles were just beginning.

Chapter 8

I was glad to get back to work the next morning, mistakenly thinking that Miguel's fling with Bianca was a thing of the past and all our family problems were resolved.

Ryan's mood was cheerful as well. A high-school English teacher, he'd spent Sunday evening grading papers and was pleased with his students' progress.

By noon, the knots in a worrisome case had been ironed out, and our receptionist and I celebrated with a long lunch after our exercise walk around the Riverwalk Mall.

The bubble burst mid-afternoon with a call from Miguel.

"You busy?" he asked.

"Never too busy for you. What's up?"

"Bianca phoned. She wants us to get back together."

"Oh."

"That's it? Oh?"

"I'm just...surprised. What made you change your mind?" *Again.*

"I haven't exactly decided yet."

A ray of hope.

"Did she have any explanation for her...behavior?"

"Yeah. It was, uh, something about her hormones."

"Well, that happens," I had to confess. "But I don't think it would affect someone's IQ."

He was silent a moment, then, "That's cold."

"You're right." I felt like blaming it on *my* hormones, but that excuse would have been as phony as Bianca's. "Off the subject—did you happen to tell Bianca that Leo's gay?"

"No. Why would I do that?"

"It's just—for some reason—when we first met her she was, uh, very nice to Ryan but snubbed Leo."

"Huh. Funny, she asked me if you all had mentioned meeting her. I told her no and didn't think any more about it."

A question flickered across my radar, then disappeared. "Oh, well, it's not important."

"Why I called," Miguel went on, "I guess I was hoping you could—I dunno. You usually see all sides of everything."

He sounded so dejected, I knew he wasn't just trying to butter me up. But my objectivity had run dry where Bianca was concerned.

"You say you're undecided?"

"Yeah. Bianca thinks I'm being unfair not to give it another chance."

"I know you don't want to be a jerk, honey, but it's just as unfair to drag it on and on if it's not working."

"I guess I'd be a jerk to end it over the phone too," he said gloomily. "I'll go back this weekend and get it over with. I'll just have to figure out how to say it. 'Be kind but be honest.' Like that's so easy."

"Not easy, but not impossible either. You'll find a way."

No matter what he said, she'd hear what she wanted to hear. No need to point this out. Besides, I felt Miguel hadn't really needed my opinion as much as he needed a listening ear—a way to nail down a conclusion he'd already reached without knowing he'd reached it.

* * *

Whatever stress might build up during our time away from Mustang Island magically lifts when we drive onto the Port Aransas ferry. Whenever the ferry docks (after our five-minute ride), we look for a fisherwoman who seems to be a fixture on the pier. Always dressed in red, she waits patiently for a catch. Beside her—also waiting patiently—is a huge brown pelican who must consider himself her pet. Every now and then she tosses him a small fish, which he catches mid-air.

Ryan and I had followed our usual pattern and skipped a weekend before going out again. We could hardly wait to take one of our long walks along the beach, watching the changing colors of the gulf and the sky.

Five weeks had gone by since Mayra's party, and we were into October now. I didn't know what was going on with Miguel. He'd gone to the Island two weekends in a row after our phone conversation, supposedly to break up with Bianca. He and Ryan and Leo had met for pizza one evening between weekends. Ryan had come home looking glum and not saying much. Apparently Miguel wasn't interested in our collective advice.

This afternoon, midway though our walk, Ryan and I saw Miguel and Bianca coming toward us. Miguel's hands were in the pockets of his cut-offs. Bianca, in a surprisingly modest poncho, had her hand tucked in the crook of his arm. Turning in another direction, they either didn't see us or pretended not to. But they'd been close enough for me to see the grim look on Miguel's face and the constant movement of Bianca's mouth. She was either chewing gum very rapidly or giving him hell.

Ryan frowned. I assumed it was because of our mutual dislike of Bianca and our displeasure at seeing that Miguel still hadn't broken loose. I wished later that I'd asked Ryan about it.

* * *

That evening Ryan and I played Mexican Train with Alana and Beto at their kitchen table. We'd been pretending that everything was normal, but our attention to the dominoes—usually loud and lively—was flat and mechanical.

Gabe had stayed with his cousin in Zapata so they could work on a car they were rebuilding. Amá, Apá, and Leo had stayed home too, so it seemed even quieter than usual.

The only sounds came from Carlos' guitar as they drifted from his bedroom into the kitchen. A beginner, he was learning one song with two chords.

> *"As I (long pause) walked out (long pause) in the (long pause) streets of La- (long pause) re-do...."*

Alana got up to take a couple of aspirin and close the bedroom door. "Patience, patience," she muttered.

Ryan tried to lighten the mood. "Just think, in a few weeks he'll be playing with Scaly and the Lepers."

Alana bopped Ryan, but at least he'd earned a smile.

Miguel came home long enough to mumble hello and disappear into the room he shared with Carlos. We could hear some arguing; then Miguel slammed out of the room.

"Mijo," Beto said sharply.

Miguel lowered his eyes. "*Con permiso*. I'm sorry, everyone."

He turned back to the bedroom, stuck his head in the door to say something to Carlos, then left before anything more could be said.

Carlos marched into the kitchen, bristling with indignation, and stood by Alana. "Why is Miguel always so grumpy?"

The dark circles under Alana's eyes betrayed her worry as she put her arm around Carlos. "I wish I knew, mijito, I wish I knew."

*　　*　　*

Back in San Antonio again, I heard from Alana from time to time, but none of us heard anything more from Miguel. Whatever was going on between him and Bianca, he chose to keep to himself.

Another two weeks went by. Ryan, Leo, their parents, and I left for the Island at noon on a Friday. The Meléndez crew came out a little later, as soon as school let out for Gabe and Carlos. Miguel came out separately, stopped long enough to say hello and leave again.

We had no inkling that our world was about to fall apart.

But Saturday dawned with Leo's gruesome discovery of Bianca's body. After waking Ryan and me, Leo agreed to the difficult task of breaking the news to Miguel. However, to add to the turmoil, Leo returned a few minutes later to tell us Miguel had left the Island sometime during the night.

Chapter 9

Sunday afternoon brought the interview with Sgt. Fay and Sgt. Bullis. As soon as they left, Ryan and I moved to the kitchen for something cold to drink.

Ryan poured a Tecate for himself and a Dr. Pepper for me. Despite my thirst, I felt as if my throat had closed up. I took a few sips of my soda, hoping it would calm the butterflies in my stomach.

After comparing notes, we were relieved to find that our answers to the detectives' questions more-or-less jibed. Then Ryan voiced the thought that worried me: "I can't tell if they've really zeroed in on Miguel, or if they were just fishing."

I shivered. "At first I thought they just wanted to talk to us because it happened here. I mean, that seemed logical. But all those questions about Miguel...."

"Sharon, there's something—"

The jangling of the phone interrupted Ryan. We stared at each other a moment before I picked it up.

Mayra Montaño was on the line. I looked at the clock. A whole four minutes had gone by since the detectives left.

"What have they found out?" she demanded.

I carried the cell phone and my soda to the front window and looked across the street, half-expecting to see Mayra staring back at me through binoculars. Maybe the sticks in her head acted as some kind of radar device, whereby she could track me from anywhere on the planet.

"Where are you?" I asked.

"At home," she said impatiently. "Lydia Wilson told me the cops were at your place."

Of course. The Wilsons, Barky's owners, lived in the cottage next to ours. They didn't even need binoculars to see the police cars coming and going.

Well, two could play this game. I was just as curious to know what the neighbors had heard. Fib a little; learn a little. I set my drink on the end table, sat down on one end of our beachwood couch, slipped off my sandals, and tucked my legs under me.

"You know how they are—the cops, I mean," I said, taking up the thread of our conversation. "They don't let on much. But—they wanted to know if we'd seen or heard anything."

She gasped. "Oh, my! Were you able to tell them anything?"

"Just that I heard a car drive by and...some other strange noises," I improvised. "This happened around three in the morning. I can't prove it, but I'm absolutely convinced that's when...when Bianca was killed."

"Is that what they think?"

"Well, of course they wouldn't say, but I got that impression. They'll be checking with the other neighbors to get their observations. Bianca's neighbors too." *Including you.*

"Yes, indeed. They were swarming all over the place yesterday morning. I told them what I could."

I swallowed hard, almost afraid to hear what she might have said. Before I could ask, she changed the subject.

"Did they tell you that wasn't Miss Bianca La Croix's real name?"

"They did, but I forgot," I lied, counting on Mayra's eagerness to sound important.

"Bertha Lumpkin. Doesn't that beat all? Miss Hot-Pants was plain old Bertha Lumpkin!"

I had to laugh at the incredulity in Mayra's voice.

She laughed too. "Mm hmm. I thought you'd be surprised."

"They asked if we knew any of the men she was seeing," I said. Crossing my fingers was getting to be a habit.

Mayra was silent a moment. "I'd hate to get anyone in trouble. Especially that nice young nephew of yours."

"Well, fortunately, Miguel was in San Antonio when it happened."

"That's what he told you?"

I swallowed down my uneasiness again. Yesterday our family had all gathered at Amá and Apá's, finding strength in our solidarity. Alana told us that Miguel had come to their cottage shortly after midnight. Unable to sleep, she'd been watching a late-night TV movie. Miguel had sat on the couch beside her, put his arm around her, and given her a kiss.

"Don't worry, Mom," he'd told her. "Everything's going to be all right."

Then he'd left, saying he was on his way back home.

"For the first time in weeks I got a good night's sleep," Alana said. "I slept so soundly I never heard another thing— not till Leo came over with the horrible news."

I could only hope Miguel left when he said he did and arrived safely in San Antonio well before the dog woke me up. I knew the police had one agenda with their broad timeline, but I had another: emphasizing the "three-o'clock" time in Mayra's mind.

Returning to her on the phone, I said, "I'm certain Miguel left here about midnight—give or take half an hour."

"Well, that fits. They sure had a row—right about then. I was in the middle of a *Golden Girls* re-run, and it comes on at twelve."

"Must have been a pretty noisy fight if you could hear it over the TV."

She snorted. "I tell you, that Miss Hot-Pants had a way of creating more drama than any television—" Mayra stopped short and lowered her voice. "I guess that sounds harsh under the circumstances. But her being dead doesn't change the way she acted."

"You're right, and it's important to remember." *Even if I have mixed feelings about hearing all this.*

"Oh, my. She was yelling and throwing things at that poor young man. He just walked to his car without saying a word."

"Did you see someone else come over there after Miguel left?"

"No," she said regretfully. "I went to bed as soon as my program was over."

"Well, *someone* must have come over later—or else she went out again."

Mayra perked up. "Of course. I did hear a car door opening and closing later on. It made kind of a creaky sound—like it needed oiling. Not too loud, just enough to wake me up. I assumed it was your nephew coming back."

"Could have been any number of people, I suppose."

"That's for sure."

I felt a surge of hope. Maybe I wasn't relying solely on intuition and rumor.

"You know, Mayra, when you said you wouldn't want to make trouble for innocent people—well, I feel the same way. But I'd sure like to find some answers on my own. Would you be willing to help?"

"Damn right! Especially if it would help your nephew!"

Chapter 10

"What are you and Mayra plotting?" Ryan asked when I joined him after our phone call. He'd gone outside and was standing at the edge of the patio, surveying the hibiscus.

"Well, she knows everybody in a three-mile radius, and she also seems to know something about other men Bianca might have been seeing. I'd like to find out something that would lead away from Miguel."

"And how are you going to go about that?"

"Oh, you know. Ask around. Talk with people...."

"That could be risky, sweetheart. What if you say the wrong thing to the wrong person?"

"I promise not to rattle anyone."

"Are you crossing your fingers again?"

I laughed. "No. I wouldn't do that to you. But I will do my best to keep a low profile and do more listening than talking."

Ryan set his Tecate on the cabana table, then took me in his arms and pulled me close. "Seems like I'm always telling you to be careful."

I kissed him softly. "Seems like I'm always reminding you my middle name is 'Chicken.' Don't worry about me...but I'm glad you do."

* * *

Ryan clicked off the cell phone. "No one answers."

"That's because they're on their way here."

Following my gaze, he saw Alana and Beto walking at a fast clip on the footpath behind the cottages. They pushed

53

through the gate and hurried up to our patio. Slightly breathless, Alana sank down on the glider and held her hand out to Beto. He sat next to her and placed a comforting arm around her shoulders. We pulled up wicker chairs across from them.

Beto's gray eyes reflected a mixture of worry and frustration. "They reached Miguel and asked if he'd come back here to answer some questions."

"Is that really necessary?" Alana demanded.

"No, not really," I said. "They could probably have the police in San Antone interview Miguel. But the more cooperative he is, the quicker he can clear his name."

Alana's normally beautiful face looked drawn, but her brown eyes flashed fire. She brushed a wayward strand of hair out of her face, then pounded her fist on the arm of the glider. "I don't know what upsets me more. The way Bianca's death affects Miguel. Or that the police think he's somehow—responsible—for it."

"Poor guy. I guess he's taking it pretty hard."

"I don't know how he's taking it," she murmured, her demeanor wilting. "We hated to break the news over the phone, but we didn't want him to hear about it some other way first. So we called him yesterday morning. He hardly said anything."

"Has Leo talked to him yet?"

She nodded. "Leo went over there as soon as he got back and called us afterwards. Miguel's all mixed up. He told Leo he didn't have any feelings for her. At the same time, he's in shock. Besides all this, he's gotten way behind in his studies."

Miguel wasn't the only one who was mixed up. Alana seemed to be going in all different directions. I thought studying would be the last thing on Miguel's mind—though obviously not Alana's. On the other hand, maybe he could get immersed in it and shut out everything else.

"At least the university is going on fall break next week," I offered half-heartedly. "So maybe it'll give him a chance to catch up."

"Not if he has to keep running back and forth to Port Aransas." The fire was back. "Besides, he's innocent, so the questioning and the extra trips are a big waste of time."

"I understand how you feel, Alana, but...people close to the victim are always the first to come under the spotlight." I didn't add that spouses and lovers are guilty more often than not, so, from their viewpoint, the police had reason for being suspicious. The fact that *we* believed in Miguel's innocence didn't carry much weight. "Did they interview you too?"

"Yes, Lt. Richmond and his sidekick nailed us to the wall this afternoon."

"Now, Corazón," Beto said, "It wasn't like that. "They were very courteous."

"And right now I bet they're checking with the guys Lt. Richmond sent to talk to you and Ryan," Alana said. "To see if our stories add up."

"Well, I'm sure we agreed where it counted," I said. "We hadn't seen Miguel since Friday night, and that's where their questions seemed to lead."

Alana nodded. "Lt. Richmond asked about time too. I told him I'd seen Miguel right before he left here—sometime after midnight Saturday. But I couldn't be any more specific than that."

"Unfortunately, Mayra Montaño *was* able to be more specific. She connected the time with a TV program she was watching—also around midnight. And she overheard a fight between Miguel and Bianca. So it might look like he was the last one to see her alive. The next-to-last one anyway."

"Sharon, I hate it when you play devil's advocate."

"Hey, I'm on your side, Alana. But you need to know— Miguel needs to know—what he's up against."

"Well, I still think their time would be better spent finding out who *really* killed Bianca."

"I'm sure they're looking at other possibilities, " I said with more conviction than I felt. "And starting tomorrow, I'm going to help them along."

Alana raised an eyebrow, but smiled in spite of herself. "I'm sure they'll love that."

"I promise to be very lovable. The thing is, they do welcome outside information. Key word: information. That's why they'll be interviewing everyone in the neighborhood. The problem is sifting through the pet theories of all the busybodies and hoping to find some worthwhile leads. Anyway, I plan to do some sifting of my own."

"Well, that *sounds* good, but how...? I mean, you can't very well go knocking on everyone's door.... Can you?"

I laughed. "No. Just Mayra's door. We're in on this together. She has a great big kitchen, with a great big round table, and a great big pot of coffee brewing day and night. People are always going in and out, so it's a logical place to get together and exchange gossip. I'll just blend in with the group and see if I can learn anything."

Beto gave me a nod of encouragement. "You have a way of getting people to confide in you. *Buena suerte*!"

Alana's eyes welled with tears as she reached over to squeeze my hand.

Chapter 11

Sure enough, the neighbors were abuzz with speculation. Mayra's back door was open when I arrived Monday morning, and I could hear lively chatter inside.

I called softly, "Hello? Mind if I come in?"

"Sharon!" Mayra feigned surprise. "You know you're always welcome!"

I smiled, pretending I did know that, as I came in and took a seat at the kitchen table. I halfway expected the hush that greeted me and the guarded looks on some of the faces around me, but it was still a little unsettling.

I had met most of the women several weeks ago at the luau, so Mayra must have assumed introductions weren't necessary, which was fine with me. Dressed in a silk muumuu patterned with bright peacock feathers, and sporting her ever-present Japanese hairstyle, she bustled around her kitchen while I tried to look inconspicuous. After she brought me a cup of coffee and seated herself, we all spent a few minutes sipping our beverages and snacking on the various sweets she'd set out.

"Isn't it terrible?" I offered at last.

Some of the women nodded.

"I for one don't think he did it," Lydia Wilson said, looking directly at me. We'd greeted each other across our back yards from time to time, so hers was one of the familiar faces here. Her gingery curls, big brown eyes, and lightly freckled face had always made me think of Raggedy Ann—cheerful and kind.

Mayra nodded approvingly. "Such a nice young man. He'd never do something like that."

It occurred to me that while dancing around the word *murder* and not naming names, we were deciphering the shorthand quite easily.

Thelma Bigelow's face mottled, the maroons, tans, and oranges engaged in serious combat. "Of course he would," she said peevishly. "Anyone can do anything if they're egged on enough."

You too, Thelma?

"She did egg people on," I agreed with a bland smile, hoping to steer the discussion from Miguel to "people."

"*Oh*, yes," Lydia said. "I heard John finally got fed up."

"You got that right," Doris Hood said, helping herself to another piece of coffee cake. Doris was round and loud, with short gray hair and large hazel eyes. "He was fixin' to fire her sorry butt."

"Bianca worked at the sales office?" I asked, trying to recall what Miguel had told me.

Doris guffawed. "If you want to call it 'work.'"

"I don't think we should speak ill of the dead," whispered Ornella Hewett. A mousy emaciated-looking woman with eyes that seemed much too large for her thin face, Ornella hadn't ventured into the conversation up till now. There was an "old-fashioned" air about her, prompted, I think, by the pinafore-type jumper she wore over a blouse with long billowy sleeves.

"I'm just makin' a plain statement of fact," Doris retorted. "Besides, you spoke plenty ill when she was alive."

Ornella retreated into her shell, leaving me to wonder what that was all about.

I supposed I could add John—whoever he was—to the growing list of people who were unhappy with Bianca. Then it came back to me. Miguel had said that Bianca came to Port Aransas to work for her uncle. Was John her uncle?

With a start, I realized I'd been so wrapped up in Miguel's problems with Bianca, and my own unkind thoughts toward her, I hadn't given any thought to the impact her death would have on her own family. Now, all kinds of questions came to mind. Had John been asked to make the official ID? Would he be the one to make funeral arrangements—whenever the autopsy was completed. How soon would that be? Weren't there other relatives who might want to take her back "home"—wherever that was?

Rather than ask direct questions, which would likely put people off, I took a stab in the dark to see where it would lead.

"I heard her sister—or maybe it's a cousin—is supposed to be here any day now."

"Where did you hear that?" Thelma asked sharply.

I felt my face turn red and tried to dig my way out with yet another fib. "Actually, it's something I *over*heard, and I could have misunderstood. I probably shouldn't have said anything."

Mayra came to my rescue. "No, I think you heard it right. At least, I heard the same thing. Can't remember where. The sister lives in Baton Rouge, I think."

"That's what I was told," someone else said. "That Bianca came from Baton Rouge. I didn't know she had a sister. Of course she never said much about her family."

Mayra stood and moved to the counter. "Mmm." She closed her eyes and breathed deeply as a beatific look spread across her face. "Smell that fresh coffee? Refill anyone?"

She didn't wait for an answer but brought the coffeepot to the table and looked around for takers.

Most of us took seconds. A couple of women said they had errands to run and made their goodbyes. About the same time, a few more women dropped in. The "swinging-door effect" brought about a change in conversation once everyone was settled in with more coffee and goodies.

"Do you live around here, Sharon?" Fina Borrego asked me. I'd met Fina at the luau—one of those people I liked instantly. She was about my age, with an open friendly face, thick curly brown hair, and green eyes. After being sidetracked by the encounter with Bianca that night, I had looked around for Fina, but she'd already left. Although I'd hoped to see her again, I hadn't exactly envisioned it happening under these circumstances.

"We live in San Antonio," I said, "but it must seem like we live here. We stay at one of our uncle's cottages—just on the other side of the mobile-home park—whenever we can get a weekend away."

"Oh, good!" She smiled warmly. "I was hoping we'd run into each other again. We had to leave Mayra's party early. Eddie—one of our kids—had a baseball game. He was pitching, so we didn't want to miss those last few innings."

"Fina has *lots* of kids," Doris put in.

Fina rolled her eyes, then laughed. "Five."

"Sounds like you enjoy them. My best friend came from a large family, and they kind of adopted me. I think they felt sorry for me, being an only child."

I didn't add that I'd felt a little sorry for myself before they took me under their wing. My mother was rather remote, and it took me years to realize that was simply her nature and no fault of hers or mine. She lives in Minnesota now, in a climate better suited to her disposition, and spends her time looking up her Scandinavian forebears on the web.

I live in a sunny climate, have no interest in my ancestors, and am blessed with a loving mother-in-law who treats me as one of her own.

Before long, the conversation drifted back to Bianca and the murder that had shocked this seemingly placid community.

"She wasn't very likable," Fina said, "but no one should have to die like that."

"You do know," Thelma said, with a touch of malice, "that it was Sharon's nephew who killed her."

Fina gasped and stammered. "No, I...I'm sorry, Sharon. I had no idea."

"Miguel didn't kill her," I said evenly, giving Thelma an icy stare. I stifled an impulse to yank off her stiffly curled wig. "He went out with her for a while, so the most he's guilty of is bad judgment."

"Good thing bad judgment isn't a crime, or we'd all land up in jail," Lydia added.

Everyone laughed, breaking the tension.

"Miguel Meléndez is your nephew?" Fina asked.

"Yes. You know him?"

"Not exactly. He and his dad came into our shop one afternoon, out of curiosity, I think. Dan—that's my husband—has a small computer business similar to Beto's. Installation, repairs, Internet-made-easy, you name it. Anyway, Dan and Beto hit it off right away. They must have talked shop for over an hour."

"What did Miguel do all this time?"

"Well, he chatted with my niece and me for a while. We work in the front office. Valerie thought he was a hunk and couldn't keep her eyes off him. I liked him because he was both friendly and respectful."

"That's the kind you always read about in the papers," Thelma sniffed. "Those polite kids have a way of turning out to be psychopaths who go around hacking up people."

"What really won me over," Fina continued, as if Thelma hadn't spoken, "was the way he treated our cat. Shadow is sort of a fixture in the office. He's seventeen years old, and mostly sleeps. Miguel petted him and talked to him, and told us about his little brother's cat."

"Psychopaths aren't usually nice to cats," Doris said as she munched a maple-frosted donut.

Lydia nodded. "Dogs either. I've seen Miguel stop to pet Barky. Barky darn near wags his tail off."

Apparently Thelma's efforts to make Miguel look bad had backfired. I figured the cause of her snit was her husband's involvement with Bianca, and was more curious than ever to find out what had gone on. I hoped Mayra would have some answers.

Chapter 12

Lydia looked at her watch. "Goodness me. It's almost lunchtime."

As everyone else was leaving, Mayra motioned for me to stay. She led us into the living room, which was decorated with Hawaiian doodads and held an eclectic mish-mash of comfortable furniture. We sat facing each other on matching forest-green armchairs.

"Well, what did you think?" she asked.

"I was going to ask you the same thing. I was afraid I'd blown it by inventing a sister for Bianca. I'm not a good liar, even when I think I'm being clever."

Mayra brushed away my concern with a wave of her hand. "It worked. That's all that counts. Miss Hot-Pants does have a sister, so it's a good guess she'd come down here."

"How did you find out about the sister? Bianca seems— seemed—to create a whole fantasy about her life."

Mayra gave a hearty laugh. "I learned quite by accident. One morning when I went in to pay my rent, John was muttering about how 'these Lumpkin girls' would do him in. Of course I didn't catch on. Should have figured it out since one of the Lumpkin sisters wasn't at her desk." Mayra's eyes crinkled in amusement at the memory.

I chuckled too. "I've been trying to think of her as Bianca instead of...what I used to call her, but I'm afraid 'Bertha Lumpkin' is too much."

"Amen. Maybe it's best to stick with what *she* liked. Poor deluded thing."

Poor deluded *Miguel*. At least he was more grounded to begin with. He would survive, but I wasn't quite ready to forgive Bianca for the hell she'd caused him. Was still causing him. Which reminded me, he was due in town this afternoon and wanted to talk with me before going to the police station.

"Shoot. I have to leave pretty soon, and I still have a few questions, if you have time."

"All the time in the world."

"For one thing, If Bianca really has a sister, why did Thelma act so suspicious when I brought it up?"

Mayra patted my arm. "Now don't you worry about Thelma. She's probably afraid Bianca's sister might know things that would point suspicion at Slim."

"Slim! That sounds like Thelma suspects Slim herself."

"I'm sure she does. And that could explain why she's so bent on blaming your nephew."

"But what would Slim's motive be?"

"Possessiveness? Not wanting Bianca involved with other men? One of those male ego things."

"The same kind of motive they'll probably pin on Miguel," I said glumly. "And it fits Thelma too—the 'possessive' part anyway."

"True. But I don't think she'd go that far. And there could be other motives for Slim—blackmail, extortion.... Maybe Miss Hot Pants just got too expensive."

I raised my eyebrows.

"Slim owns a car dealership. Rumor has it his business dealings are what you might call a little shady. I don't know for sure, but I think Bianca unearthed something. What I do know is, the beginning of every month, she exchanged one top-of-the-line car for another. The latest was a Jaguar XJ. Red."

"Miguel's Jeep must have been a come-down!"

"Oh, I doubt that mattered. The fun would be keeping Slim on a string."

"Does he live nearby?"

"Well, I guess everybody in Sonrisa Vista lives fairly near everybody else. The Bigelows live on the last street—Number 33, I think.

I tried visualizing where their home might be. I recalled that the park was built in a rectangle—four parallel streets with ten lots each that were bisected by a cross street. Beyond the last street were the clubhouse, swimming pool, and a small playground. Two side streets completed the rectangle. But until now, I'd never been in anyone's home but Mayra's—Number 6—which was on the corner in the middle of the first street.

"Didn't you say Bianca lived—used to live—two doors down from you?"

She nodded. "Hers was Number 8, John lives in Number 9, and the office is Number 10. The Borregos live in Number 40—the last place on the last street, right across from the playground—and—oh, my, here I go—you're not interested in all this, and no reason to remember it all anyway."

She was right. My mind was still stuck on her own street. "Who lives right next door to you—between you and Bianca? It seems like they'd have heard—or John would have heard—all the, um, arguments going on between Miguel and Bianca."

"Orville Edwards—you remember the elderly gentleman who has an eye for all the ladies? He lives in Number 7. Once he takes his hearing aids out for the evening, it would take more than Bianca's histrionics to wake him up."

"And John?"

"Poor John. He's a dear, and he took it pretty hard when the police brought him the news."

"Even though he and Bianca didn't get along?"

"Well, you never expect something like that."

"True."

"He came over here after they left to tell me about it. They'd asked him if he'd heard anything, of course, but he couldn't help. You see, he was getting over the flu. Gloria, I think it was, had been in the office that afternoon, and she said he looked terrible—coughing and all that. She told him to go home and take care of himself."

"And that night?" I said, guiding Mayra back to the subject.

"He started taking something for the fever, and it made him groggy. He heard Bianca yelling all right, but before he could get up the energy to come out and tell her to keep it down, he heard the door slam, so he figured she'd gone inside."

"Did he hear Miguel drive away?"

She frowned. "He didn't mention it, and it didn't occur to me to ask. I figured we'd each seen and heard the same thing."

I sighed. "Here I said I needed to leave, and I'm still here trying to sort things out."

We stood and walked back through the kitchen.

Mayra paused at the door. "Come by whenever you can, and we'll sort all you want to."

I hugged her. "Thanks. I'll see you soon."

Chapter 13

Miguel arrived at their family cottage about half an hour before I got there. Ryan had come over shortly afterwards, since Alana was expecting us for lunch.

Miguel looked drawn, as if he hadn't eaten or slept the past couple of days. He said he didn't have much appetite, but took a few bites of his chicken-salad sandwich under Alana's watchful eye.

She kept popping up and down to wait on us, whether we needed it or not, and her fidgeting began to rub off on us.

After the fifth time she looked in the fridge for more ice cubes, Ryan said, "Alana, light somewhere."

Beto went over and put his arm around her. "Come sit down, Corazón. We have plenty of everything."

She sat down then and asked me—again—if I didn't think I should go with Miguel.

"He'll do fine. They're just interviewing him as a possible witness. Not as a suspect." *So far.*

"No last-minute words of advice?"

"Just what I've already told him. Be respectful. Tell the truth but don't elaborate."

A wary look crossed Miguel's face, and tiny beads of sweat broke out on his forehead. I took his hand, which felt cold and clammy. "*Dímelo*, Miguel. What's bothering you?"

"What do you think they'll ask?"

"When you last saw Bianca. Where you went after that. What was that last fight about."

"Y'know, I've changed my mind. I would like you to go with me."

I hesitated. We both knew it would be better if he started out on his own. He could always ask for a lawyer later if he felt he needed to. But he must have had a good reason for asking me.

"Do you have to leave right away?" Alana asked. "You hardly touched your sandwich."

He stood and gave her a hug. "I'd like to get it over with. I'll eat a huge dinner tonight. Promise."

We left before Alana could offer any more objections.

* * *

"Will they be back from lunch yet?" I asked Miguel as we drove toward the police station in his Jeep. "It's just a little after twelve-thirty."

"I hope not. I need to talk to you—and I didn't want to do it around Mom and all her worrying."

"You think I don't worry about you?"

He gave me a half-smile. "Yeah. I know you do. That's why I didn't go into this before. But I think you can handle it better than Mom."

He stopped in front of the station, turned off the motor, and stared at the steering wheel.

I folded my hands in my lap and tried to look nonchalant. "Would it help if I played devil's advocate?"

"Yeah." He looked at me, a mixture of caution and relief in his eyes.

"Okay, for starters, when was the last time you saw Bianca LaCroix?"

"Saturday night. We went out and I brought her home."

"Saturday night will do. That's all I asked."

"Right."

"Neighbors said they heard a loud argument when you brought her home. What was that about?"

His jaw tightened. "It's not.... Do I have to answer that?"

"Why wouldn't you?"

"It's personal."

"Nothing's personal anymore where Bianca's concerned."

He didn't answer.

"Look, Miguel, keep it simple. I can guess. You talked about breaking up. Right?'

"Okay, simple. We talked about breaking up."

"Whose idea was it?"

"Are you kidding?"

"I'm the devil, remember? And you better speak nicely to me."

Another small grin. "It was mutual."

"Not a good answer."

"You win. My idea."

"How did she take it?"

He shrugged. "She wasn't pleased."

My turn to grin. "Classic understatement. You're catching on. Did she try to threaten you?"

"She made a lot of noise. I quit listening."

"Did she eventually agree to break up?"

He shifted uncomfortably. "No."

"So your problem wasn't solved. How did you plan to get rid of her?"

"Sharon, I'm talking to you as Sharon now. I didn't really give a damn whether she agreed or not. I was tired of her lies, and she didn't have a hold on me anymore, so I just walked away."

"Okay, I'm talking to you as Miguel now. What hold?"

He was silent a few moments. "She told me she was pregnant. I found out she was lying. That's really what the fight was all about."

I pressed my fingers against my temples. Something was missing here, and I was almost afraid to find out what it was.

Chapter 14

"Let me think a minute," I said. We were both quiet for a while, looking straight ahead instead of at each other. I finally turned back to Miguel.

"Let's back up a bit. What if you simply told the police you were tired of her lying. That's pretty straightforward and a logical reason to end a relationship."

He looked at me, despair written all over his face. "What if they ask for specifics?"

"Well, wasn't there more than one lie?"

"Huh! Let me count the times."

"Could you name some that weren't so...explosive?"

"Probably, but the little ones wouldn't matter. And the serious ones, that's what they'd ask about. What if they want to know how I found out she wasn't pregnant?"

"How *did* you find out?"

"Uncle Leo hacked into the computer at the hospital and dug up some confidential medical records."

"What?"

Miguel scrunched down in his seat and studied the steering wheel again.

I leaned back and took several deep breaths. "Oh, god, we sure don't want to go there!"

"I know."

"How come he decided to do that in the first place?"

"It's a long story. And everything's all jumbled."

"Take your time. No, wait. When are you supposed to see Lt. Richmond?"

"Sometime between one and two. I told him it depended on the traffic."

And now we had something more serious than traffic to worry about. I couldn't believe Leo had taken such a risk.

"I guess," Miguel spoke at last, "it goes back to when she wanted to get back together again and I came here to talk it out. I told her we shouldn't drag it out if it wasn't working." He looked at me out of the corner of his eye. "Sound familiar? That was your advice."

"Guess I'll have to take down my shingle."

"Nah, you were right. It just fell on deaf ears. But then she said something way out." Miguel mimicked Bianca's little-girl voice: "'Your Uncle Leo put you up to this, didn't he!' I told her I didn't know what she was talking about. I guess she could tell I really didn't.

"So then she got all nicey nicey and said she was sorry, it was a 'hormonal thing.' She used that excuse a lot. Anyway, she said it was worse now that she was pregnant. That's about the way she said it. Blew my mind."

"Did you believe her?"

"Yeah. I guess. I thought she was on the pill. But that's what I thought she was lying about—lying about taking the pill. Not about being pregnant."

"So when did her comment about Leo start to register?"

"After I got back home. I had a lot of time to think."

"And a lot to think about!"

"You said it. She'd asked me about Uncle Leo before, and I remembered you'd said she acted odd around him. So I decided to ask him. I told him the whole story. Him and Uncle Ryan both. That night they came over for pizza. Uncle Ryan clammed up, and I don't know what he thought. Uncle Leo just seemed kinda sad."

Miguel swallowed hard. "Anyway, he didn't remember ever having seen her before Mrs. Montaño's luau. But it made him suspicious that she brought it up so many times. The only thing he could think of was that there was some connection with the hospital. Somehow she must have known he was a nurse there. Maybe she remembered seeing him even if he didn't remember seeing her."

Maybe she'd noticed Leo's good looks after all, I thought cattily.

"He thought she sounded bi-polar," Miguel continued, "and maybe she'd gotten some kind of treatment or evaluation there. He looked for a record on her, but he couldn't find anything on a 'Bianca LaCroix.'"

"I see. So then, how did you find out her real name?"

"I can't believe I was so dumb. Whenever I went to the sales office, John would call her Bertha, and she'd get mad, and he'd apologize and say old habits died hard, or something like that. She told me later it was a nickname one of her nephews had given her because he couldn't say her name right. Sounded logical to me."

"It's not that far-fetched. Little kids have a way of mangling names."

"Yeah. Carlos used to call me 'Meow.'" Miguel grinned at the memory, his features softening momentarily.

"So you told Leo her real name?"

"After it finally dawned on me that might be the link. Problem was, I didn't know her last name—then. But Uncle Leo looked up all the Berthas in the database, and that's when he found her."

"How could he be sure he had the right Bertha?"

"He wasn't at first. There was a picture, but she had brown hair. The more he looked at it, well, he was convinced. Besides that, the chart said she came from Baton

Rouge, and that fit. The age didn't fit—thirty-six—but that was two years ago. She'd told me she was twenty-eight, and I believed her." He hit the steering wheel with his fist. "Dumb."

"You're not dumb. You had no reason to doubt her when you first met." I paused. "Why was she in the hospital?"

Miguel looked out the window, then back at me. "She'd had a botched abortion. Not at Uncle Leo's hospital. They don't do them there. But at some cut-rate clinic. She lost a lot of blood. Probably came close to dying. Someone found her unconscious and brought her to Santa Rita."

For the first time, I saw pain and grief in Miguel's face, reminding me that Bianca was someone he'd truly cared for not so long ago.

"She came out of it," he said, "but she could never have kids."

Also for the first time, I felt the tiniest inkling of pity for Bianca. Maybe this whole experience had left her mentally and emotionally unstable as well. Or maybe I had it backwards. Maybe she had a mental disorder to begin with. I just wished Miguel hadn't gotten caught up in her lies or delusions, whichever they were. And I hoped and prayed Leo wouldn't get caught for accessing restricted information.

I touched Miguel's shoulder, and his composure finally broke. He crossed his arms on the steering wheel, cradled his head on them, and shed silent tears.

Chapter 15

Several minutes later, Miguel sat up straight and made an effort to pull himself together. "Where do we go from here? I can't tell them all that."

"Ordinarily I'd never advise someone to lie. It usually backfires. *But* I'm going to make a suggestion, and you can take it or leave it."

"What's that?"

"You could say that one night while you two had had a little too much to drink, she let her real name slip. There's no one to prove that happened, but no one can disprove it either. And it's a simple lie, not a complicated one. You could also say—and this part is probably true—that you got to doubting other things she'd said, like how she was a world traveler and so on. And you felt used."

Miguel thought that over. "What if they ask when and where?"

"The drinking? Her place? Does she keep any booze there?"

"Yeah. We didn't barhop. I'm underage, remember?"

"Okay. That leaves 'when.' Be vague. A few weeks ago. Three or four. Five or six. Something like that."

He folded his arms across his chest. "What were her exact words?"

"You can't remember. Don't try to think of something. You don't want to sound like you've memorized it."

"Did we get drunk every weekend?"

"Good thinking. You do your own devil stuff very well. Let's just scrap the lie. Not a good idea in the first place. But the truth is *Bianca* wasn't truthful. I think you can get that across without bringing in Leo."

He rubbed the back of his neck. "I'll bring in Carlos' cat instead. Spot's smarter than I am. He saw through her right away."

"Very funny. Okay, try this. The earlier fight when Thelma Bigelow showed up and accused Bianca of fooling around with her husband. You can say this made you see an ugly side of Bianca. One thing, neighbors overheard that scene, so it can be verified. Not that it should be necessary."

Miguel relaxed a fraction. "That might work."

"Think you're ready to go inside now?"

"Ready as I'll ever be."

"Don't forget to ask for a copy of the interview tape."

"I won't." He leaned over and gave me a big hug. "Thanks, auntie."

I hugged him back. "What's an auntie for?"

He got out of the Jeep, then turned and rested his arm on the window frame. "Keys are still in the ignition. Why don't you drive home, and I'll give you a call on your cell when I'm finished here."

"I'll be waiting. Good luck."

*   *   *

I felt achy when I got back home. Didn't know if it was from sitting too long in the Jeep or from the underlying tension in our conversation. I went out on the patio and eased myself into a cushioned chair. Ryan gave my shoulders and neck a gentle massage before sitting next to me.

"How'd it go?" he asked.

"I didn't go in with him after all. He just wanted to talk over some things first. Things he'd already told you and Leo. Bianca's so-called pregnancy, for one."

"Yeah. I started to tell you yesterday. I'm afraid it's not going to be much of a secret after the autopsy…. Wait a minute. What do you mean, 'so-called' pregnancy?"

I relayed what Miguel had said.

"I'm surprised Leo didn't tell me."

"I'm guessing he didn't have a chance. Everything happened so fast! Leo must have found out while he was at work—sometime Friday—and told Miguel that evening after he got here. Once Miguel was off the hook, he confronted Bianca and didn't look back."

"Then Saturday morning she was found dead."

"And only yesterday we were talking to the Hardy Boys. Seems like eons ago."

A cool breeze swept across the patio, and the temperature took a sudden drop.

Ryan looked up at the darkening sky. "I guess this is the beginning of the storm they predicted."

How convenient, I thought. Weather to match every mood.

Chapter 16

Ryan and I picked up Miguel at the police station when his interview was over. He was quiet on the way to his family cottage, where we dropped him off. Thirty minutes later he showed up at our place.

"Mom and Dad were worried, so I told them, 'Hey, look, they didn't arrest me.' I guess it helped that I was home again and not in handcuffs. This whole thing has bothered Gabe and Carlos too. Especially Carlos. I don't want him scared I'm going to jail."

"You think the interview went okay?" Ryan asked.

"I dunno. I have a copy of the tape. I'd like you to hear it, but I'd rather you didn't mention it to anyone else."

We sat down at the kitchen table while Miguel played the tape for us. We had to listen closely, and it was frustrating not to see facial expressions or body language. Every now and then, I'd ask him to pause the tape to get a clearer picture in my mind.

First were the standard preliminaries—names of victim, interviewer, and interviewee, place, date and time of the session. Next came a few remarks apparently intended to put Miguel at ease (or catch him off guard). After that, they got down to the nitty gritty.

"When did you see Ms. Lumpkin last?" Lt. Richmond asked.

"Friday night."

"What time?"

"I left her place about 11:30, I think. 11:45. Close to that."

"What did you do then?"

"I went back to San Antonio. Well, first I stopped by my parents' to let them know I was leaving."

"When did you get to San Antonio?"

"I dunno. Four a.m.?"

"Took you four hours?"

"More or less." (pause) "Probably less. Let's see. I stopped for coffee at a truckstop near Sinton."

"Anyone remember seeing you there?"

"I doubt it."

"Did you get a receipt?"

"I only spent a couple of dollars. If I got a receipt, I didn't keep it."

Miguel sounded a tad cranky. I hoped it didn't come across that way to Lt. Richmond.

"Okay, back to Friday night," Lt. Richmond resumed. *"You spent all evening at your girlfriend's place?"*

"No. We went to a concert on the beach."

The next part sounded garbled. I asked Miguel to rewind a short space.

He complied, color creeping up his neck. "It sounded bad enough the first time. I told him we'd gone to hear *Grungy Sleaze*."

"Sorry. It wasn't clear."

The tape replayed the mumbled part and continued on.

"We came back to her place about 9:30 or 10:00," Miguel said.

"Neighbors heard you arguing."

Miguel gave a muffled snort. "Yeah. It got a little loud."

"What was it about?"

(pause) "We decided to break up."

"We?"

"Well, we were still working on it. She wasn't ready to end it yet."

"How come?"

(pause) "She wanted to give it another try. I thought we'd already given it about 40 or 50."

"That many?"

"I guess not. Three or four maybe?"

"Did you know she was pregnant?"

"No."

I asked Miguel to pause the tape again.

"My god, Miguel. Do you think Leo could have been wrong? Or was Lt. Richmond just trying to rattle you?"

He shook his head. "I didn't take time to analyze it—I was too startled to say anything but 'no.'"

"He must have realized you were telling the truth."

"Yeah, I probably looked as shocked as I felt."

We turned the tape back on.

"She didn't tell you?" Lt. Richmond asked.

(pause) "What she told me—she said she was on the pill."

"She told other people she was pregnant. Why wouldn't she tell you?"

"I don't know what to say. She lied so much, I don't know what went on in her mind."

"What did she lie about?"

"Her name, for one thing."

"How did you find that out? Looked at her driver's license?"

"No. I should've. We went someplace one night where they carded us. She got real mad and made us leave rather than show 'em her license. I couldn't understand it. You'd think she'd be flattered they thought she looked that young."

"Well, how DID you find out?"

(pause) "I asked her why she was so pissed, and that's when she told me."

"Just like that?"

"Well, not at first. I kept asking her. She—uh—she finally told me. Kinda made a joke about it."

"I think you're leaving something out."

We paused the tape again, and I gave Miguel a stern look. "What was that all about?"

"The part about her not wanting to be carded was true. But I figured there wasn't any way he could check out whether I'd asked her about it or not. So I decided to make up my own lie." Miguel lowered his gaze. "He's sharp. I could tell he didn't believe me, so I dropped it."

I could picture Miguel squirming, his discomfort giving him away. We turned the tape on again.

Miguel exhaled deeply before continuing. "I found out she made up lots of stuff about herself. Told me she'd traveled the world and spoke lots of languages. I believed it all till my dad asked her some questions and you could tell she was full of it."

"Didn't that piss you off? Her making a fool of you like that?"

81

"Well, yeah. I felt pretty stupid. But I thought she had a bigger problem than mine if she had to lie all the time. I felt like I never really knew her."

"Do you think she was seeing someone else?"

(pause) "I got that impression."

"Isn't that really what you fought about? You thought she'd been cheating on you?"

This was followed by silence. Miguel told me that idea was so far out, he couldn't come up with anything to say, so he'd just shaken his head.

"You sure you weren't jealous?" Lt. Richmond asked.

"I'm sure."

"Would you be willing to take a polygraph?"

(pause) "I'd rather not."

"How did he react to that?" I asked Miguel.

"He didn't. He just told me to keep myself available, and that was pretty much it."

Chapter 17

It was drizzling when I hurried over to Mayra's the next morning. By now, more than being curious, I felt almost desperate to learn about Thelma Bigelow's husband and was glad Mayra had offered to explain what was going on between him and Bianca.

I hoped the gloomy weather would keep the coffee bunch in their respective homes. No such luck. I saw five or six neighbors already gathered around Mayra's kitchen table when I peeked in the door. *Guess if people have to stay inside on a rainy day, they might as well do it at Mayra's*, I groused to myself. I shook raindrops and frustration from my umbrella with equal vigor.

As I came inside, welcoming smiles and hellos both warmed me and made me ashamed of my single-mindedness. It was true—as we'd told Sgt. Fay and Sgt. Bullis—that we hadn't known our neighbors except to wave to and exchange a few pleasantries. But now, one by one, I was meeting women I liked. How ironic, I mused, that I was making new friends while trying to unmask a murderer.

The lone exception to the aura of camaraderie was Thelma Bigelow, looking her usual blotched and sour self. I wondered if she only came to make sure no one talked about her behind her back.

I seated myself next to Lydia Wilson, while Mayra, clad in a bright purple caftan, beamed and brought me a steaming cup of coffee. I stirred in creamer and made a mental note of the faces around me. No-nonsense Doris

Hood was sitting on the other side of Lydia and enjoying a raspberry-filled croissant. Doris could be blunt and tactless, but there was an honesty about her I found refreshing. And yesterday she'd said something that made me wonder if Bianca had seduced Ornella Hewett's husband too.

How many other husbands? With a start I remembered Bianca's remark about someone else—who was it? I'd tucked the name away in my memory, and now it wanted to stay tucked. It had to do with Bianca's nails, her manicurist. Shouldn't be too hard to pin down. Mayra might know.

"Sharon, I'd like you to meet my sister-in-law, Gloria Bullis," Fina Borrego said, introducing me to the young woman sitting next to her.

"Bullis?" I squeaked, then cleared my throat and tried again. "I'm glad to meet you, Gloria."

No one seemed fazed by my awkward reaction, and everyone slipped into a lively conversation about books and movies. I wondered what they'd been discussing before my arrival. Still, I began to relax. Gloria seemed open and likable and—I told myself—might not even be related to the Sgt. Bullis of the Port Aransas Police Department.

That hope was dashed when Lydia innocently mentioned a mystery novel she was reading. Count on Thelma to use this as an excuse to ambush Gloria.

"That reminds me," Thelma said, looking at me, "does everyone know Gloria's husband is investigating Bianca LaCroix's murder?"

A startled silence followed, then Doris asked tartly, "Lydia's book reminded you of Gloria's husband?"

Thelma glared at Doris. "The truth is, we're all more interested in what's happening here in our town than in Lydia's book."

I had to agree with Thelma there, if only silently. Maybe they'd avoided discussing Bianca's murder *because* of me, which kind of sabotaged my plan to learn anything at Mayra's kaffee klatches. On the other hand, maybe I was sabotaging my own plan: I hadn't counted on taking a genuine interest in the people here.

Thelma turned to Gloria. "What have they found out?"

"Gee, I don't know," Gloria said smoothly. "Don never discusses his cases with me."

Did I see her cross her fingers?

"Well, I don't know why they're dragging their heels," Thelma snapped. "It's obvious the Meléndez boy did it."

"Really?" Gloria countered. "You must know something the police don't."

"Those people always carry knives," Thelma muttered under her breath.

I was speechless, but Gloria didn't skip a beat. "*Mujeres estúpidas dicen cosas estúpidas*," she said softly, with an angelic smile.

I almost choked on my coffee. "I thought my brother-in-law knew every dicho in existence. But there's one I've never heard,."

"That's because I just made it up, but your brother-in-law is welcome to add it to his collection."

By then, everyone but Thelma was chuckling.

"It's really rude, Gloria," she carped, "to speak in a foreign language that not everyone understands."

"You're right. What it means...." She paused and I held my breath, wondering if she'd repeat, "Stupid women say stupid things."

"What I meant to say," she continued, "have you shared your concerns with Lt. Richmond?"

"I told your husband and that kid-partner of his when they were asking around, for all the good it did."

"Then I'm sure it'll reach Lt. Richmond's desk. If not, I'll see to it myself."

I figured Gloria must have some reason for pushing this, but it put my nerves on edge. What if Thelma had actually seen or heard something that could appear damaging to Miguel? What if Gloria's friendliness toward me was superficial after all?

Mayra suggested we get back to discussing books, but I found it hard to concentrate. After a while, I made excuses to leave, deciding that my absence might make for less inhibited discussion should the subject of Bianca's death come up again. Mayra could always fill me in later.

* * *

On impulse, I decided to take a cue from Gloria and go see Lt. Richmond myself. Ryan had gone with Beto and Carlos early that morning to tour the Lex. I left Ryan a note and drove to the police station. The rain was falling in earnest now. Strange, I thought as I squinted through the frenzied windshield wipers, that the weather hadn't even been mentioned at Mayra's. I supposed people who lived here year 'round took it in their stride. Or—more likely— Thelma was right. Murder was more on everyone's minds right now. Such a rare occurrence here was bound to produce some degree of apprehension, as well as a kind of morbid fascination.

The receptionist, Shelley Northrup, relayed my name to Lt. Richmond and assured me he could see me if I didn't mind waiting fifteen or twenty minutes. I figured that should give me just enough time to question the wisdom of what I was doing and back out.

Ten minutes later Lt. Richmond stepped into the foyer and introduced himself. I guessed him to be in his mid- to late-forties; tall and good-looking, with dark piercing eyes and black hair just barely sprinkled with gray.

We went into his office, where we exchanged a few cordial remarks before he asked me what was on my mind.

"I'm Miguel Meléndez's aunt, and I'm concerned that he's been connected with Bianca—Bertha Lumpkin's—murder."

"And you believe he's innocent?" Lt. Richmond asked, not unkindly.

"Yes. I know that's what family members always say...."

"You're more than family, though, aren't you? Aren't you representing him?"

The question took me aback. But of course he'd know I was a lawyer from all the information we'd given the police earlier.

"No. I hope he won't need 'representing.' If it comes to that, well, that's not the kind of law I do."

"I see." Lt. Richmond leaned back in his swivel chair, his hands behind his head, and waited for me to say why I was here.

"Have you questioned anyone else?" I asked.

He studied me a moment. "We have a few leads." Police talk for "It's none of your business." Then he leaned forward. "Darn few. Do you have any suggestions?"

I looked away, then back at him. "No. Only suspicions— just like everyone else, I guess. Gossip. Blah blah blah." Suddenly I felt like crying, the last thing I wanted to do here.

"For what it's worth, your nephew impressed me as being pretty straightforward—mostly. But he's hiding something."

I looked away again. "He doesn't want it to come up about his drinking—the bars he's gone to where they serve minors."

"Now *you're* hiding something. And we already know all about those places."

I felt my face turn red. "It doesn't have anything to do with.... Well, it does, but not—"

He waited.

I stood to leave, hooked the strap of my purse over my shoulder, and thanked him for his time. "I'm not sure this was one of my better ideas."

He walked me to the door. "Don't give up. Every now and then, there's a grain of truth in gossip. If you find one, let me know."

I looked up to see his eyes twinkling, and smiled in return. "Will do."

Chapter 18

The rain was falling almost sideways now, and the umbrella kept trying to blow away on my mad dash from the carport to the back door. I'd gotten home damp and chilled, but glad to see that Ryan had arrived safely too. Drying off and snuggling into my fluffy old robe helped dispel my anxiety, but didn't chase it away altogether.

"He must have thought I was a complete idiot," I told Ryan while we sat in the living room and sipped hot chocolate after a late lunch. I'd indulged by adding extra marshmallows in mine, hoping that would cheer me up.

Ryan leaned back in the recliner and propped his feet on the footrest. "What did you do that was so idiotic?"

"Well, I tell that nice receptionist—Shelley—that I *really* need to talk to Lt. Richmond. I make it sound kind of urgent. Then when I get in there, I change my tune and don't say anything relevant. I might as well have talked about the weather."

"What were you planning to say?"

"I'd planned to go in and tell him to investigate Slim Bigelow, Thelma's husband. Then it hit me that I had absolutely nothing concrete to go on, and I'd probably sound just as petty and spiteful as Thelma."

"Honey, I think you're being too hard on yourself. Did Lt. Richmond tell you to quit being an idiot and never darken his door again?"

I laughed. "No. In fact, he gave me permission to snoop. Or that's the way I choose to interpret it."

*   *   *

Amá and Apá had invited the family for dinner that evening. Amá said that regardless of storm, stress, or strife, people had to eat. Right now, "family" didn't include Miguel and Gabe, simply because they'd gone up to San Antonio together that morning. They'd always been close, and though Miguel didn't say so, I suspected the Island held too many memories of Bianca and he needed to get away, even if it meant making several trips here and back.

"Family" did include Apá's brother Tío Roque, however. The brothers had similar facial features—which Ryan and Miguel had inherited—and iron-gray hair. There the resemblance ended. Tío Roque also had a bushy gray mustache and wore square black-rimmed glasses.

We saw him from time to time whenever we stayed on the Island, but he was usually busy maintaining the various properties he owned. On the other hand, whenever he did have spare time, he enjoyed Mayra's company. Amá phoned me to say he'd even asked her if he could invite Mayra to join us for dinner. He said she'd often had him over for home-cooked meals, and he seldom had a chance to return the favor.

"Then he went on and on about what a good cook I am," Amá said. "Like I couldn't see through that."

I laughed. "But it's true! You're the best."

She laughed too. "I have to confess it pleased me. *Pero* I told him we probably wouldn't be very good company."

"She won't expect us to be. But I think *she* will be good company. She's kind-hearted and funny."

"*Pues*, since my brother-in-law thinks so, I guess it's high time we met. We weren't here for her luau."

As it turned out, even though we called it an early evening, Mayra did provide us with the diversion we needed.

True to form, she was dressed in a gold and black tunic, patterned with exotic jungle cats, and gold slacks. Her black hair was in its usual bun, graced by its usual chopsticks.

We sat around Amá and Apá's dining table with its forest-green tablecloth and ivy-patterned dinnerware. We relished every bite of Amá's chicken enchiladas and pico de gallo, and Mayra conceded that Amá *might* be the better cook. Amá modestly declined the title, and Tío Roque wisely refrained from choosing sides.

As a gust of wind rattled the windows, Amá nervously asked Tío Roque, "Do you think this storm will turn into a hurricane?"

He patted her shoulder. "The weather report is still calling it a tropical storm, Ysela. And it's due to land farther down the coast—but close enough that we're feeling the effects."

"We'll get plenty of warning if anything changes," Mayra reassured her. "I think it's the charged air that makes us feel a little edgy."

Good. Something to add to the list of things making me edgy.

"The last time a hurricane seemed really close," she went on, "I sat cross-legged on the floor of my bathroom, huddled together with my niece and her husband, their three kids, five dogs, and six cats. One of the kids had a cell phone with a camera and got some delightful pictures of our 'imprisonment.'"

Why predicaments like this seem so comical in retrospect, I don't know, but Mayra's story had us all laughing, and the rest of the evening went by on a lighter note. Before leaving, she invited Amá and Alana to drop over for coffee "anytime." I hoped we could all take her up on it when the storms, both our own and Mother Nature's, were over.

I planned to skip the kaffee klatch for a day or two, not because of the storms, but in hopes Mayra could glean some helpful information if I wasn't around. At the same time, I thought it would seem odd if I quit going altogether. What a pickle I'd put myself in.

*   *   *

Tío Roque said we could stay in the cottages as long as we liked. Not only that, he insisted on lending us his Kia so we could have an extra car whenever we needed it. So Ryan and I decided to stay at least till fall break was over, unless the weather got worse. In the meantime, I was able to keep in touch with my office online.

Ryan's parents, along with Alana, Beto, and Carlos, all went back to Zapata the next morning—Wednesday morning.

"You know something," I remarked to Ryan over breakfast. "Why haven't I thought to ask Tío Roque what he knows about Bianca and the men she might have been involved with?"

"Why don't you give him a call and see if we can get together and talk it over?"

Two hours later, after braving the rains that showed no sign of letting up, we were in Tío Roque's office downtown. Since his part-time secretary wouldn't come in till later, he suggested we sit in the reception area, where we could face one another around the coffee table.

"Bertha, or Bianca, or whatever she called herself, was a real piece of work," he said, shaking his head. "I hated seeing Miguelito get mixed up with her, but I figured he'd wise up sooner or later."

"You're right. He did," Ryan said. "But they had a nasty fight when he tried to break loose, and now the police think that's a motive for murder."

I winced, hearing Ryan voice it so bluntly, but knew we couldn't afford to tiptoe around it.

"Pretty thin motive, if you ask me." Tío Roque grimaced. "I wish she'd never come here. Poor John. We've been friends a long time—ever since 'Nam. He used to tell me his troubles with Bianca when we'd had a Tecate or two. She'd sold him some hard-luck story, and he thought he was doing her a favor to let her come work for him."

"What went wrong?" I asked.

"She didn't know the first thing about office work—or didn't care—or both. Got people's rent mixed up. Took money out of petty cash. Didn't try to hide it, just acted like it was her due. Then she'd get her back up whenever John complained."

"Did John know anything about the men she was seeing? Someone besides Miguel?"

"He didn't name names that I recall. He did say one time she just used men to satisfy her ego—that they were 'interchangeable.' I think that's the term he used."

"Then I'm surprised she didn't dump Miguel. She sure had him wrapped around her little finger at one time."

Tío Roque shrugged. "Maybe he beat her to it." He shook his head again. "Now John is having to deal with her sister. She's a royal pain, but in the opposite way."

"Like—how?"

"Oh, how did he put it. Self-righteous. Bitter. Cordelia is several years older than Bertha and ugly as a mud fence—I'm quoting John here. Resented the fact that Bertha was pretty. They grew up in a very strict so-called 'religious' home. The hell-fire and damnation line suited Cordelia, but Bertha rebelled."

Once again I felt a pang of sympathy for Bertha/Bianca.

"Is Cordelia here in Port Aransas now?" Ryan asked.

"Yep. Got in yesterday afternoon. Had a bumpy flight. Expects to get stranded here in the storm and hasn't quit bitchin' about it. I had the pleasure of meeting her when I stopped by John's office to see how he was doing. I bet you'd like to meet her too," he added, peering at us mischievously over his black-rimmed glasses.

"Can't wait," Ryan said.

"To tell you the truth," I said, "I *would* like to meet her and John both. I have a feeling I'd learn something helpful. I guess that sounds a little self-serving, but, well, it is."

"It's 'Miguel-serving,'" Tío Roque said. "And maybe I can help."

Chapter 19

"Cordelia and John are packing up Bertha's things," Tío Roque continued. "We can go over there, say we wanted to see if we could take them out for lunch, or bring them something."

"You're sure it wouldn't seem awkward? Or a little insensitive? Wouldn't they wonder why we didn't just call?" I asked.

"Not around here. People are always dropping in to see their neighbors without calling."

Thinking of Mayra's open house, I took him at his word.

"As for sensitivity—Cordelia has all the sensitivity of a cement mixer," he said. "Come on. I'll take you over there."

*   *   *

Sloshing through and around rain puddles, we hurried from Tío's car to Bianca's front door. John ushered us in, looking relieved at the interruption, and hung our raingear on a coat rack in the foyer. His soulful brown eyes reminded me of a basset hound, and I wondered if the deep lines creasing his face were recent.

Cordelia's scowl and downturned mouth broadcast her reaction loud and clear. Except for this, she didn't look quite the mud fence I'd expected. Her face was flushed, but whether this was her natural skin tone or due to her irritation with us, I couldn't tell. Like Bianca, she'd bleached her hair, which hung straight to her shoulders. Her eyes were the same shade of blue, though they bulged slightly.

My general impression was one of a blowfish about to explode.

Tío made introductions as if she'd hung out a big "Welcome" sign.

"We know what a difficult task this is, and we thought it might help to take time out for lunch," I said, pretending she'd be delighted at the idea. "We could get a sandwich at Little Joe's."

"Good, we could use a break," John said at the same time Cordelia was saying, "No thanks."

John turned to her. "Aren't you hungry? We've been at this since eight o'clock and it's nearly twelve-thirty."

"Go on without me," she said in a martyred tone. "The sooner I finish up here, the sooner I can get out of this godforsaken place."

I smiled sweetly, no longer feeling guilty for intruding. "We could bring something here, if you'd rather."

"I wouldn't rather."

"Then could I help you with the packing, Cordelia? Not with any of the personal stuff, of course, but maybe with the dishes and cookware?"

She regarded me suspiciously, as if caught between her desire to finish the task and her desire to get rid of me.

"Nice of you to offer," John said, "but we can't accept."

"She didn't ask you." Acid dripped from Cordelia's voice. "I could use a little help around here."

John winked at me, and I tried looking disinterested.

"Where shall I start?" I asked in a neutral tone. I doubted if I could uncover anything revealing about Bianca in the Tupperware, and Cordelia hardly seemed the conversational type. But my offer indicated my level of desperation to find answers.

* * *

We worked quickly and quietly for the next half hour, the only sound the growling of my stomach. The guys had left for lunch, and I kept thinking of the barbecue I was missing. *Well, you asked for it*, I chided myself.

Bianca had a lot of cookware in pristine condition, making me wonder if she ever used it. The coffeepot and mugs were the only things that showed any signs of wear. I picked up a cup depicting the dunes against a sky of delicate pinks, golds, and lavenders. As I traced the cool ceramic with my fingers, I was caught up in an unexpected wave of sadness and an eerie sensation I couldn't quite identify—as if I were invading her privacy somehow.

Cordelia apparently realized I wasn't going to chit-chat or ask nosy questions and was the first to break the silence. "Were you a friend of Bertha's?"

"Not really. I guess you could say we were on friendly terms, but I didn't know her very well."

"Then why are you here?"

I almost dropped the mug I was handling, then set it down carefully. I was quiet a few moments, turning over possible answers in my mind. At last I said, "We were visiting our uncle. He and John are friends, and he thought maybe you all would like to join us for lunch. Then when we got here, it looked to me like you could use an extra hand."

I finished wrapping the mug and placed it in the packing box while she stared at me.

"I don't think she had many women friends," Cordelia said, turning to wrap up a pitcher.

Careful. Careful.

"You reap what you sow," she continued bitterly.

"That happens."

Still, Gloria's words echoed in my mind: *No one should have to die like that.*

"I tried to warn that girl, but she just laughed at me, and now she's earned a place in hell," Cordelia stated with a self-satisfied air. "'The wages of sin.'"

I picked up another cup, this one with an intricate design of bluebonnets intertwined with gaillardia. "For all we know, she had a change of heart," I said.

And for all I know, I was born to be devil's advocate.

"I thought she was pretty nice," I went on, mentally crossing my fingers. I shouldn't have stretched it, but it's so tempting to lie to people I don't like.

"You didn't know her like I did!" Cordelia practically spit the words at me. Her ruddy face became even redder, and a vein pulsed in her forehead.

I began to worry she might have a stroke. "That's true. I was only around her once or twice."

Cordelia sat down at the kitchen table, pulled a tissue from her pocket, and wiped her face. I sat opposite her, not knowing what to say or do next. We'd finished packing up everything in the kitchen, except for the curtains and some pictures on the wall that had come with the mobile home.

"She ruined my life," Cordelia stated.

Both the accusation and its abruptness caught me up short.

"I see."

"No, you don't see. You have no idea."

I nodded, then shook my head, hoping one or the other gesture would be the appropriate response.

She stared out the window with the raindrops pelting against it.

"For twenty-four years I've hated her."

"Oh. Um."

She turned away from the window and pinned me with her gaze.

"I was nineteen years old, engaged to Ernie Thibodeaux. He was everything to me. She was only fourteen, but she seduced him. I knew she was brazen, but I didn't think he'd be taken in."

"That's.... Oh, my.... No wonder."

Despite my fumbling words, she heard the distress in my voice.

"Once she'd taken him away from me, she dropped him. Ernie tried to win her back, but it was no use. He just sank deeper and deeper into despair. Not long afterwards, he killed himself."

I was too shocked to respond.

She sighed heavily. "Ernie was weak. But she was cruel. It was a game with her, and I saw her play it time and again."

"John seemed to think she wanted to change," I murmured, placing my hands in my lap where I could cross my fingers unnoticed.

"John's a fool. Was a fool. I think he wised up when the rumors started."

"Rumors?"

"You don't live here, do you."

"No, we just come down on weekends now and then."

"John told me all the men she was linked with. That he knew about, of course. There were probably others."

The venom had returned to Cordelia's voice, sending a shiver up my spine. I don't know what I expected. Here I'd hoped to dig up dirt on Bianca's "conquests" but hadn't stopped to think how the dirt would splatter back on me.

"I'm going to unpack one of those glasses we wrapped," I said. "I need a drink of water."

"You do look a little pale. I set some paper cups aside. You can use one of those. Look in the cabinet to the right of the sink."

I found the cups and filled one with tap water, which I drank slowly, wishing I had some Maalox to go along with it. When I sat across from Cordelia again, she began spewing out a number of names. Oddly enough, Miguel's wasn't among them. The only ones I recognized were Bigelow, Hewett, and Borrego. Fina's husband? Surely not. My stomach took an extra turn.

Cordelia paused, her eyes glittering. "Your husband looks familiar. He wasn't one of them, was he?"

I shook my head. "That's strange—that he looks familiar, I mean."

Had she confused him with Miguel? Another case of mistaken identity? How much did she know—about Miguel and Bianca, about the police investigation, about Ryan and me? I supposed it helped that Miguel's last name was different from ours. Cordelia certainly didn't seem one to mince words if she'd made any connections. Still I couldn't help prodding. "Maybe you saw my husband on your last trip to Port Aransas."

"That's impossible!"

I shrugged. *Why was it impossible, and why did she answer so quickly?*

Chapter 20

Cordelia's face flushed. As if reading my mind—or my shrug—she made an explanation of sorts. "There was no 'last trip.' I've never been to this hellhole before and I wouldn't be here now if I didn't have to be."

I gave a faint smile and went on prodding. "Well, at least we know you've never seen my husband before. I guess he just has one of those familiar faces."

Cordelia snapped her fingers. "I know what it is. I saw his picture. In Bertha's photo album."

"That's—that's hard to believe."

"Are you calling me a liar?"

"No. I'm just surprised, that's all."

"Looked a lot younger, but it was him all right."

Something else didn't add up. Obviously it was Miguel's picture she'd seen, but when and where? She'd just said this was her first—and only—trip to Port Aransas. I was sure the cops had searched Bianca's place and couldn't believe they'd have overlooked a photo album. Something almost as good as a diary. "I suppose the police still have the album," I reasoned aloud.

Cordelia opened and closed her mouth a couple of times. I couldn't help thinking this mirrored her whole attitude toward me: open one minute, closed the next. One big eggshell walk on my part. Maybe hers too.

"It wasn't much. Just a little booklet, really," she said. "They found it in her night table and returned it to John yesterday. He gave it to me to pack away."

"That's good. I'm glad you had a chance to look at it first."

Again I got the fish-mouth reaction before she made up her mind to speak. "Well, of course I was curious to see why it would be so important to the police."

"Of course. I'd be curious too. Would you mind if I looked at it?"

I'd pressed my luck too far.

"Yes, I would mind. What business is it of yours?"

"Well, you thought my husband's picture was included."

"It's packed away," she said with finality.

"That's just as well," I said. "Good to put the past behind you."

Anger flared in her eyes. "What do you mean?"

What button had I pushed? "Nothing. I didn't mean to upset you." But I couldn't resist pushing again—on purpose, this time—if I could only grasp the right straw.

"I can understand why you don't want to look at the album again," I said. "It must remind you of the way she betrayed you."

Bingo.

"The little slut had kept pictures of Ernie. *My* Ernie!" Cordelia's voice rose as her face contorted. "After all these years, she still had his pictures. She had no right."

"No right at all! You know what I'd've done? I'd have taken those pictures out before the police got hold of them!"

She blinked then, her lids closing and opening quickly over her bulbous eyes.

My cell phone rang. Ryan's ring. I picked up my purse from the counter where I'd left it, and pulled out the phone.

"Hope we haven't been gone too long," Ryan said. "We thought it might give you a little more time to worm something out of whatserface.

I pressed the receiver closer to my ear, hoping "whatserface" couldn't hear Ryan at the other end.

"That's great! Now that you mention it, I *would* like some lunch. Let me check with Cordelia." Holding the phone to my chest, I turned to her. "They're bringing back some take-out. What would you like?"

"Filet mignon."

I chuckled, pretending her sarcasm was meant as a joke, then put the phone to my ear again."

"Anything sounds good," I told Ryan. "I'll be glad to see you."

"Me too you. I take it you can't talk now, but did you learn anything?"

Yeah. I learned she's lying about something. "No. We're at a stopping point." *In more ways than one.* "See ya soon!"

* * *

Despite her determination to be difficult, Cordelia couldn't resist the barbecue beef subs the guys brought from Little Joe's. After we'd eaten, we all pitched in to box up the rest of Bianca's things. Cordelia all but barred us from the bedroom, while she swooped Bianca's clothes and costume jewelry into large black garbage bags to be hauled to the dumpster.

"Even the second-hand stores wouldn't touch this trampy stuff," she asserted as she shoved the bags from the bedroom into the living room, where the rest of us were working.

Once again I felt an indescribable sadness, as if Bianca had somehow been violated. "Isn't there someone in your family who'd like a memento? A charm bracelet or something?" I asked. *Isn't there anyone to mourn her?*

John cleared his throat. "Aren't you being too hasty, Cordelia?"

If the bags hadn't been so heavy, I think she'd have thrown them at him.

"Do whatever you like," she said icily. "I've done all I can, and I intend to take the next plane out of here."

The three men looked at one another.

"I guess you haven't heard the news," John said. "The storm made landfall down near Port Isabel, and we'll be lucky if all we get is wind and rain. All flights out of Corpus are cancelled indefinitely."

Chapter 21

The look Cordelia gave us held more fury than any tropical storm—as if we were somehow responsible for her delay in getting out of "this hellhole."

Tío Roque glanced around at the stacks of bags and boxes and smiled amiably. "It looks like we've finished here, so I guess we'll be on our way."

"If you think I'm staying another night in that hotel you put me up in, John Addison, you've got another think coming. The staff was rude."

"You can stay at my place," he said wearily.

"And try to sleep on that lumpy excuse of a couch? No thanks. I'd be awake all night."

"You know what," I suggested as I took our raincoats off the coat rack. "We didn't pack away the phone books. You can look through the Yellow Pages and see what's available. With the weather like this, all the hotels might be full, but it's worth a try."

She gave me another dark look. "How could I tell I wouldn't be getting another fleabag?"

John finally rallied. "If you didn't like the Moonlit Sands, you won't like any of them. It's that or the lumpy couch. Take your pick."

By now the rest of us had donned our raingear and were heading out the door, battling the wind that wanted to shove us back inside.

"*Hasta luego*," Tío Roque shouted above the storm. "Have a nice evening!"

*   *   *

By late afternoon, the storm seemed to be tiring of us as it continued on its inland track. Still, there was enough wind and rain to remind us that the weather could be capricious whenever it chose. If what we experienced now was "merely" a remnant of the storm, I was glad we'd been spared the full brunt.

Being home with Ryan was soothing in itself. We'd agreed not to talk about the day's events until we'd had some time to ourselves. It wasn't till later in the evening that those events insisted on surfacing in my mind.

We were snuggled together on the loveseat, eating popcorn and watching *Barney Miller* on DVD when Ryan squeezed my shoulder and said, "I can almost hear those wheels turning in your head. Tell me."

He sensed my mood so often, I no longer questioned it. And I knew he was curious about my day, so we stopped the player while I told him everything I could remember.

"She quotes the Bible one minute and spews hatred the next. It's scary, Ryan. *She's* scary. She's obsessed...."

"You think she could have killed Bianca?"

"I think it fits her personality."

"Then why would she wait all these years?"

"Twenty-four years, to be exact. I was surprised she didn't add months, days, and hours. But you're right. Why wait? Do you suppose finding those photos of her ex-fiancé could have sent her over the edge?"

"When do you think she found those pictures to begin with?"

I mulled that over. "I see what you mean. I can't picture her coming down for a 'friendly little visit,' accidentally discovering them, then stabbing Bianca and going home. I think she came down some other time, but doesn't want to admit it for some reason."

"So she could have found the pictures earlier, then gone home, thought it over, and come back in the middle of the night—I don't know, honey. Bianca's murder doesn't sound like something Cordelia would have planned. Remember what Leo said?"

"Not really." All I remembered was Leo's steering me away from Bianca's blood-stained body.

"Well, he said she'd been stabbed in the heart, which was what killed her. If that had been the only stab wound, there wouldn't have been much blood. But there was a lot of blood on her abdomen, even though it had pretty much congealed by the time he found her."

Ryan watched me closely. "Are you okay with this?"

I nodded, and he went on.

"Anyway, Leo said it was hard to tell underneath all the blood, but he saw just two or three stab wounds—more like slashes. He thought it was strange. The wound to the heart was precise. The others seemed haphazard. He didn't know what to make of it."

"You're right. I think that leaves Cordelia out after all. I think she'd have enjoyed stabbing her sister over and over again—certainly more than two or three times""

"Hey, you sound pretty bloodthirsty. I think Leo overestimated your weak stomach."

"I do have a nasty view of Cordelia, don't I."

"Yeah, but there's some basis for it.... Something else. Because of the way the blood was smeared and the body positioned, Leo doesn't think Bianca was killed where they found her.

"Ooooh! Now that puts a whole new spin on everything! Maybe Cordelia killed Bianca in that bedroom she didn't want us going into, then dragged her over to where she thought Miguel lived. Probably in Bianca's car."

"Cordelia would have to be pretty strong to do all that, wouldn't she?"

"Maybe." I thought that over. "Maybe not if she wrapped her sister's body in a plastic bag and slid that as much as she could."

Ryan looked doubtful. "Well, even if it happened that way, I'm sure she would have cleaned the bedroom thoroughly. And I'm sure the police would have discovered bloodstains, if any."

"Seems like it. But still...do you think I should say anything to Lt. Richmond before Cordelia leaves town?"

"Think it through, and you can decide tomorrow morning."

* * *

First thing the next morning, I called John and asked him—casually, I hoped—if this was Cordelia's first visit to Port Aransas. He told me she'd come through last summer on her way to Mexico.

"Just for a few hours," he said. "Seemed longer."

So why did she say this was the only time she'd been here?

"Well, this trip has to be a strain on you both," I said.

"Everything's a strain with Cordelia. If there's not already a crisis, she'll invent one."

"At least the storm has let up. The airport is probably open again."

"God, I hope so. We're going down there in a few minutes so she can badger the ticket agents in person."

I made some sympathetic comments, and we ended our call.

Next I made an early appointment with Lt. Richmond. This time I'd given more thought to what I wanted to tell him.

Taking Tío Roque's Kia, I drove over to the police station. Shelley greeted me with a friendly smile when I arrived. Evidently she hadn't gotten word that I was an idiot. After Lt. Richmond and I were seated in his office and had exchanged the usual greetings, I plunged right in.

"Have you met Bianca's sister, Cordelia?" I asked.

"Yes."

"Did you talk to her—interview her?"

He looked at the ceiling. "We expressed our condolences. We asked a few questions."

"She hated Bianca."

"Maybe so. But she was five-hundred miles away when—Bianca—was killed.

"Maybe so."

His eyes narrowed.

"Please hear me out. I'm not just putting up a smokescreen." I related the gist of my conversation with Cordelia, the discrepancies in it, how she'd nursed a grudge for so many years. "I'm sure she saw that photo album before you all found it. Were all the pictures there?"

"Hold on a minute. What photo album?"

"The one you found. The one you all gave back!"

He shook his head.

"Hmm. You didn't find it in her night table?"

"If it had been there, we would have found it there."

I thought that over. "Okay, maybe there was never any album to begin with. Or maybe she saw it some other time and took it home with her. Either way, I don't understand why she'd lie about it. But that's something else that bothers me—another lie she's told. She said she'd never been here before, but John says she has." I stopped to take a breath. "Can't you at least check on her whereabouts last week?"

He didn't answer at first, and I suspected he was determining the amount of the red tape it would take to chase down my wild goose. "You think," he suggested mildly, "she'd wait twenty-something years to get even with her sister?"

Now that I'd made my case, Ryan's objections came back to me. I sighed. "She really doesn't seem like the type to wait. And, to tell you the truth, I think if she did snap, she'd want to make Bianca suffer. Torture her in some way." I swallowed hard. "I'm not sure I can see her driving five-hundred miles in the middle of the night, stabbing Bianca a few times, and then hurrying home."

"Sounds like you're defending her now."

"Not exactly. Bad habit of mine—seeing all sides of something. Irritates my family to death."

He grinned. "There are worse habits. Tell you what. I'll talk to Cordelia again before she leaves town."

Chapter 22

I didn't envy the airline personnel trying to reschedule Cordelia's flight. On the other hand, I hoped it would take *lots* of rearranging to accommodate her. Long enough for Lt. Richmond to "have a word," as they say in those British movies.

After leaving the police station, I made a couple of quick calls: First to Mayra to ask for the name of Bianca's beauty salon. Mayra knew the name of the salon, but not the name of the manicurist. Next I called Ryan to tell him I was getting my nails done.

"Take your time," he said. "I met our neighbor Tom Wilson over garbage."

"Pardon me?"

"We were both taking out the trash and got to talking. Pretty interesting guy. Anyway, now that the weather's cleared, we decided to play tennis. We're on our way to the courts now."

We ended our call, and I drove over to Wanda's Waves, glad to see a sign announcing that walk-ins were welcome. As soon as I saw the names of the two manicurists, I remembered Marlene's and asked for her.

"She's busy right now, and there's two more ahead of you," the receptionist told me. "But if you're in a hurry, Florence can see you now."

"How about if I make an appointment and come back later?"

"Suit yourself." She took my name and scheduled me for right after lunch. In the meantime, there didn't seem much point in going home, since Ryan was off tennising with our neighbor. Instead I decided to do more sleuthing. Maybe Tío Roque could think of a way for me to actually *meet* the various men whose names were linked with Bianca's.

I called Tío on his cell and tracked him down at one of his cottages. I drove over there and found him taking pictures of the damage an uprooted tree had done to the carport.

"Do you have a minute?" I asked him.

"Sure, mijita."

"Meeting Cordelia was so much fun, I thought you could introduce me to some more folks connected to Bianca."

He gave a hearty laugh. "Anytime!"

"Actually, I wanted to find an un-obvious way to do this." I explained that Thelma Bigelow's husband, Slim, and Ornella Hewett's husband—I didn't know his name—had come up in conversation at Mayra's, and I'd like to see for myself what they were like.

"Slim is a wheeler-dealer car salesman. I guess you could act like you wanted to check out some new cars. Keith Hewett is an insurance agent. A good one. In fact, I need to see him about this—" Tío Roque waved his arm in a wide circle to take in the general area affected by the storm. "He said he'd be in his office this morning."

Tío Roque looked at his watch. "I was going to email him these pictures, but I can plug into his computer instead. Go with me?"

*　*　*

My initial impression of Keith Hewett was of a quiet, unremarkable man about fifty, with pale gray eyes and thinning sandy-colored hair. But when Tío Roque introduced us, Keith stiffened almost imperceptibly.

I smiled. "I'm glad to meet you. I had the pleasure of meeting your wife at Mayra Montaño's." It came out sounding a little formal, but I wanted to be upfront about knowing Ornella.

"Yes, she mentioned it."

He gave a reasonable imitation of a smile, offered me a chair, then lapsed into silence.

"Well," Tío Roque said after a few awkward moments. "I know you're busy, Keith, so we won't keep you long. I thought we could look at these pictures and decide where to go from here."

And I'll just exercise my overactive imagination while you two are busy. Although a link between dull Keith and flashy Bianca seemed unlikely, I conjured a possible scenario. Bianca would definitely like the challenge of someone who seemed immune to her advances. And maybe Keith, flattered by her attention, would give in. Or maybe not. Either way, Ornella Hewett would resent Bianca's hypothetical efforts.

"I'm going to stretch my legs." I rose and began ambling around the office, looking at various documents, awards, and pictures on the wall.

Though Keith appeared to be studying Tío's digital photos, he kept giving me quick furtive glances. I decided to escalate his nervousness a notch.

"Excuse me," I said looking directly at the two men, "Would it disturb you if I use my cell phone?"

They looked puzzled that I'd even asked, but I wanted to be sure that Keith noticed. I turned away and continued walking around the room, hoping he would think I was using the phone to take pictures. To tell you the truth, I didn't see anything out of the ordinary—nothing "picture-worthy" in my opinion. I hoped I'd rattled Keith just the same.

"We're about done here, mijita," Tío Roque called out, somewhat louder than necessary.

I turned to find Keith walking toward me. He looked displeased, but short of being angry.

"Did you reach your party?" he asked.

"Oh, I was just texting my husband. I wish I could do it as speedily as the teenagers do these days," I said cheerily as I slipped the phone back into my purse. "I was also admiring this redfish beauty you caught." I pointed to a photo of a grinning Keith standing on the dock, posing with his catch.

Keith relaxed and actually smiled at me. "You fish?"

"No. My father-in-law and Roque are the fishermen in our family. But I enjoy hearing the tales of the ones that did or didn't get away."

We chit-chatted about fresh-water versus salt-water fishing for a few minutes, then said our goodbyes.

On the way back to the cottage where I'd left my car, I peppered Tío Roque with questions about Keith Hewett.

"He seemed very suspicious of me at first. What do you think brought that on?"

Tío Roque scratched his head in bewilderment. "He certainly didn't seem like himself. Maybe Ornella told him you're a spy."

Despite the joking way he'd made this last remark, I wondered if that's the way I'd appeared to Ornella. All of a sudden I had started showing up at Mayra's for coffee— timed with Bianca's death and Miguel's supposed involvement in it.

"Did he think my 'spying' might turn up something?"

Tío Roque shrugged. "What's there to turn up?"

"Exactly!"

"You're on the wrong track, mijita. Keith's as honest as they come."

"Maybe in business. But what about his personal life? Do you think he was cheating on his wife? Specifically—with Bianca?"

He thought that over. "I doubt it. Keith carries John's insurance too, so he'd see Bianca at one place or another. Bianca flirted with anyone in pants, but that doesn't mean she followed through. Not with Keith anyway."

Well, it was clear Tío was going to defend his friend, and I respected him for it. But I wasn't convinced of Keith's innocence.

Chapter 23

I barely had time to stop for a Whataburger before my appointment with Marlene. I still hadn't thought of a subtle way to bring up Bianca's name and said a quick prayer that opportunity would knock.

I arrived at Wanda's a few minutes early after all, and found Marlene finishing another manicure. It gave me a chance to study her while ostensibly looking through a fashion magazine. I guessed her to be about my age. She had short black hair that curved around her face in a style reminiscent of the twenties—a style that was making a comeback, according to the magazine I was flipping through. It was a perfect complement to her heart-shaped face.

But her eyebrows were what caught my attention. She had waxed off her God-given brows and painted on some new ones—shaped like upside-down U's—well above their natural setting. Her amber eyes were framed by thick black lashes, and I knew I'd have to focus on those once I was seated in front of her.

When my name was called, Marlene put me at ease with a friendly smile. She began our session by removing my nail polish, then having me place my hands in a shallow bowl filled with a sudsy liquid designed to soften the cuticles. I wondered briefly if it was dishwashing soap.

While waiting for me to soften, she asked who had recommended her.

"One of my neighbors—Mayra Montaño."

"Hmm. I know who Mayra is, but she's not one of my customers."

"Well, when I asked her, yours was the only name she mentioned. I suppose she heard about you from someone else. All I know is, you were highly recommended."

I couldn't very well cross my fingers while they were in the goop, but since I'd had to wait in line for an appointment, I decided there must be some truth in the statement even if I didn't know her recommenders.

Marlene lifted my left hand from the softener and began pushing away the cuticles. "So you live near Mayra? Isn't that right by where that—that woman was murdered?"

I nodded, then lowered my voice. "They found her in the street practically in front of our cottage."

Her beautiful eyes widened, causing her eyebrows to rise to improbable new heights. "How ghoulish!" She paused briefly before returning to her task. "Well, I tell you one thing. Someone did us all a big favor!"

She jabbed my cuticles with greater fervor. A word of advice: Never agitate your manicurist when she's wielding a cuticle trimmer.

"Ouch!"

"Oh, I'm sorry!" She massaged my fingers gently. "I really am. I just get so—I *am* sorry."

"It's okay. Bianca seemed to have that effect on people." I lowered my voice further. "My nephew was dating her for a while, and our whole family was—well, you can imagine."

"I certainly can! Your nephew?" She looked up at my face, apparently assessing my age. "The kid?"

"That's the one!"

"Yeah. We saw them together a time or two. She really seemed to like him. We were hoping he'd keep her from targeting anyone else. Here, let me have your other hand."

I gave her my right hand, returning the left to the suds.

"You'd think so," I said, "but you won't believe this. The first time I met her, we were at a party, and she actually came on to my husband when I was standing right there!" I didn't have to fake my irritation at the memory.

"No kidding! Well, join the club. Oops, there I go again." The jab was less pronounced this time, maybe because I appeared to be a kindred spirit. "See Helen over there?" she waved the trimmer toward a hair stylist who was giving someone a perm. "Miss Bianca made a pass at Helen's Roy and my Al at different times. We read our guys the riot act. I told Al if I *ever* caught him fooling around, I'd cut off his cajones with a rusty razor blade."

Gruesome as Marlene's threat sounded, I wondered if Bianca had a more likely threat of her own. What if she'd convinced Al she would let his wife know about his "fooling around" in return for something—money perhaps? Would that have been motive enough for him to kill? And if not Al— or Roy or Keith or Slim—who else might "Miss Bianca" have been blackmailing?

Marlene dried off my hands and began trimming my nails. "Would you like a French manicure?"

"Sure. My hands are in your hands." *Ugh. How corny could I get?*

She smiled despite my corniness. "It works both ways. I guess it's silly to let Bianca get to me—especially now that she's gone. But it's nice to talk to someone who understands."

"I agree. The thing is, I can't help wondering if she was all talk and just enjoyed toying with people. Making men think she was hot for them, and making women jealous. Pretty sad way to live."

"Trust me, she was more than just talk. But I guess it doesn't matter anymore. Now it's our little storm that's taken over the front-page news."

She'd sparked my curiosity about Al and Roy, but I thought it wisest to go along with the subject change and chat about inconsequential things. *For now, at least.*

*   *   *

I called Ryan from the parking lot in front of Wanda's, glad to find that he'd returned home. "I'm on my way to buy a new car."

"Say what?"

I explained that I'd learned from Tío Roque that Slim Bigelow was a car dealer—and from Mayra that he was a letch—and I wanted a chance to meet him in person.

"Are you out of your mind?" Ryan asked.

"Probably. Here's the plan. I babble with Slim about getting another car. After a while, I say I need to talk it over with my husband and give you a call. Then you come and we both babble."

"I'm not into babbling."

"Okay, just show up and be grumpy."

"I'm not grumpy either. Sharon, have you thought this through? You want to meet him because you think he might have killed Bianca. Right? Don't you think that makes him a little dangerous?"

Gulp. "It's broad daylight. I'll be careful. Besides, you're going to show up and be not grumpy."

"If I don't hear from you, I'll show up in twenty minutes anyway." He paused. "You're not serious about a new car, are you?"

119

"Maybe I will be by the time I've met with Slim," I teased. "We might have to talk trade-in. Your car or mine?"

"He might recognize Tío's Kia, so I guess you'd better take mine."

"Good, I'll come change cars with you."

"But you better not get rid of it," he grumbled.

"I won't, but we have to fake it. And while we're at it, let's pretend it's *my* car."

"Should I tell him 'the wife' needs a new car?"

I laughed. Ryan knew how much that label irritated me.

"Oh, by all means," I said. "On second thought, maybe I'm jumping to conclusions. He might not be as chauvinistic as I've imagined him." *I hope not as lecherous either.*

Chapter 24

"Slim's Car Emporium Domestic and Imports New and Formerly Owned No One Undersells Us" was much larger than I'd expected. I parked in the area designated for customers and figured I'd start at the showroom. Once there, a thin young man who looked to be in his twenties accosted me.

"Are you Slim?" I asked, reasonably sure he wasn't.

"No, ma'am. I'm Jesse Bob. Did you need to see Slim?"

Well, yeah. "No, that's okay," I said, thinking fast. "I'm supposed to meet someone here." I looked at my watch. "Late again. I'll just look at a magazine while I'm waiting."

His eyes glazed over as his hopes of a commission evaporated, but he came to long enough to show me the lounge and offer me coffee. "Let me know when your friend gets here."

I smiled and nodded and picked up a leaflet at random. Turned out to be one of those religious tracts that gloats over the perceived shortcomings of everyone else's religion.

Before I could reach for something more edifying, I saw that another customer had caught Jesse Bob's attention. Now would be a good time to wander around the car lot in hopes of catching Slim's. I had noticed security cameras everywhere, so assumed it wouldn't take long before he spotted me.

Sure enough, within minutes, a porky man with a florid complexion came bounding over to greet me, rubbing his hands together in anticipation of an easy sell—or maybe an easy something else. He appeared almost bald from a distance, but as he grew closer, I saw that his crinkly reddish-blond hair was simply cropped close to his head. There's only so much odor that spearmint gum can hide, but at least he'd left the cigar behind.

He was dressed in a dark suit that was way too heavy to wear in this balmy weather. I supposed this meant his office was air conditioned to the max. He pulled a large white handkerchief from his breast pocket and wiped the sweat from his forehead before extending his other hand.

"Slim Bigelow here. They call me 'Slim' because I'm not."

He laughed heartily at his joke. I wasn't sure if I should laugh too, so I simply smiled and shook his hand.

"I hope you can help me," I said demurely. "I've had my old car for about six years now, and I'm ready for something new, but I don't know where to start."

Slim put his handkerchief away and grasped my hand in both of his, assessing me with beady eyes and shifting the gum to his other jaw. "You've come to the right place, little lady."

"I'm so grateful," I cooed. "I want something a little— jazzier—than what I have now."

"Mm hmmm. And what are you driving now?"

Ryan's car. Don't forget, Sharon. "A Saturn."

"I bet we can find just the thing for a pretty lady like you. Let's look a couple of rows over."

He placed his hand on the small of my back and guided me there while I tried not to squirm away.

"Oh, my," I exclaimed, wide-eyed at the large selection. "I'd like something in red this time. I'm tired of the same old blah white." *If you only knew, Slim. My Honda is white too.*

Slim's ever-present smile broadened, if that was possible. By now I must have convinced him I was a "typical" clueless female whose only knowledge of cars was limited to color.

We walked past a few cars till we came to a bright crimson model.

"I happen to have this classy little Sunfire here...."

I ran my fingers over the shiny hood, pretending to be interested.

"This is nice, but I was thinking more along the lines of a Jaguar."

Slim stuck his hands in his pockets and shifted the gum again. His eyes narrowed, but his smile stayed in place. "I had one. A red one. But—strangest thing—it got impounded. Maybe you heard about that?"

My mouth dropped open. I wasn't surprised it had been impounded, but I was surprised he'd bring it up. And why on earth would he think I already knew? More fast thinking. "Get *out*! I did see someone driving a red Jag, and I liked it. That's what made me think of buying one for myself."

"Could I interest you in something else?" Slim asked in a monotone.

"Well, sure. Just so it's red."

"Sunfire's all I've got."

"Isn't that a red car over there?" I pointed to a Corvette in the next row.

"Too many miles on it."

Just then, true to his word, Ryan showed up. Had twenty minutes gone by already?

Jesse Bob accompanied him, looking somewhat dazed. "He—uh—was trying to find you. Were you—ah—was someone else—"

I realized I'd led Jesse Bob to believe I was expecting "a friend" when Ryan arrived. Poor Jesse Bob. Was he worried that a jealous husband might cause trouble? Did he have to deal with jealous husbands on a regular basis?

"Oh, thank you, Jesse Bob," I said.

To Ryan, I added, "I got tired of waiting."

Relieved, Jesse Bob hurried away, leaving our threesome to fend for ourselves.

"Sorry I'm late," Ryan said, picking up the hint. He smiled in a way that always melted my heart but did nothing for Slim's.

I introduced the two men, who shook hands, reluctantly on Slim's part.

"Have we met?" Slim said. "You look familiar."

Uh oh.

"I was thinking the same thing," Ryan said evenly. "The wife and I go to the Elks Club sometimes. Was that it?"

Slim looked more closely at Ryan, evidently realizing he was too old to be Miguel, and dismissed the idea.

"Nope. Must be mistaken."

"Slim was showing me a red Sunfire," I said.

"Just remembered—it's sold."

"Oh, that's a shame. Was that the only one?"

"Afraid so."

"Well, darn. We'll just come back another time."

Slim walked us back to the entrance of the lot. He didn't exactly push us out, but we got the message just the same.

Chapter 25

Ryan and I walked back to our cars without saying much. I'm sure Slim's surveillance cameras weren't equipped with sound, but seeing them pointed at us stymied any effort at conversation.

Ryan got home a minute or two before I did and started a pot of coffee. As soon as I came into the kitchen, he put his arms around me and apologized for showing up before I could learn more from or about Slim.

"Don't feel bad. Slim had already clammed up."

"You sure? You look kind of down."

"Well, I was hoping he'd say something incriminating. Goodness knows what."

Ryan poured our coffee, and we sat at the kitchen table. I stirred creamer into mine, wishing my thoughts would organize themselves as smoothly as the creamer blended into the beverage.

"So what did happen?" Ryan asked.

"The minute I said I was interested in a red Jag, he turned the tables on me. I was looking for some kind of reaction, but that's the last thing I expected."

"Did you think he'd start twitching or foaming at the mouth?"

"Okay, laugh. But I did think he'd look startled or clench his teeth or raise his eyebrows—maybe stammer a little bit. *Something.* Anything. Then I figured he'd either try to downplay the connection to Bianca's car, or pretend not to notice. But instead he put *me* on the defensive." I told Ryan the gist of our conversation and how my plan had backfired. "Obviously, I wasn't very subtle."

"I wonder if they found anything when they impounded the Jaguar."

"I wonder too. Sometimes I think the things I don't know outnumber the things I do."

"Why don't you write 'em both down?"

"There'd be a pretty skimpy *What I Know* list. I'd have to label it *Lots of Speculation*."

"Don't discount your intuition, Sharon. You know more than you think you do."

"Well, now you've inspired me. Or maybe it's just the coffee revving me up." I stood and kissed him on the top of his head.

After taking my cup to the sink, I retrieved my laptop from the living room and set it up in the kitchen. Ryan moved his chair next to mine so he could watch the screen with me.

"Okay, let's talk this out," I said as I settled down to work. I opened a new folder, calling it *Sherlock Salazar*.

"I'll create two documents for now," I told Ryan. "One for things we don't know, and one for things we do. Then I can switch back and forth between the two while we're discussing it."

In the *Don't Know* category, I typed, *What was found in Bianca's car?* Turning to Ryan, I asked, "Do you think she might have been killed in her own car?"

"Remember, it's really Slim's car—has dealer's plates and all that. Piece of cake to trace it back to him. Might explain why he got so uptight when you got so specific."

"Makes you wonder what he's worried about. Hmm. What if the police found bloodstains?"

"Whatever happened to the knife?"

I added our questions to the list.

"I have another," he said. "What showed up in post-mortem? Any evidence she fought back? Stuff under her fingernails?"

"And if she didn't fight back, why not? Was she caught off guard because she trusted her attacker?"

"Was she drugged?"

"If it was a crime of passion, why were there so few wounds? If not, why kill her at all?"

"Was the killer interrupted?"

"Why did he—or she—leave Bianca's body in our yard?"

I finished typing what we'd questioned so far, then re-read it. "Did we leave anything out?"

Ryan shrugged. "Probably. But that should be enough for now."

"Good idea." I switched documents and labeled the new one *What We Think We Know*.

"Sounds very lawyer-like."

I wrinkled my nose at him. "Where shall we start?"

"You heard a car drive by about 3:00 in the morning. I think that's when Bianca was left in our yard, no matter how the police stretch their timeline."

"I think so too. Whatever time it was, Leo says she was already dead."

I typed in our conclusions, then asked, "What now?"

"Suspects—Who and Why."

Number One—Slim Bigelow, I typed. *Car salesman. Supposedly having a fling with Bianca. 180-degree change in behavior when he thought I was asking about her Jaguar.*

"Slim name, slim lead," Ryan said.

"It's all we got.

"Who's next?"

Keith Hewett, I typed. *Insurance adjustor/agent (?) Acted suspicious when I showed up with Tío Roque—as if he's hiding something.*

"Now I know why you didn't label this *Concrete Facts*," Ryan said.

"Yeah—it gets even murkier from here on out. Those are two of the names Cordelia linked with Bianca, courtesy John. If she was even telling the truth. She also mentioned the name 'Borrego.' I hope she didn't mean 'Dan.' He and Beto got along great when Beto visited his computer shop. And I like Fina—Dan's wife—a lot."

"Not a good reason to leave him off the list."

"Okay, I'll list him in a very small font. Along with Marlene's husband, Al, and Helen's husband, Roy. Bianca made a play for them, but I don't know if they followed through."

"Maybe we should just call this list *What* Else *We Don't Know*."

"You're right." I sighed. "Maybe this is a big waste of time."

Ryan leaned closer and put his arm around my slumping shoulders. "I didn't mean to discourage you. In fact, we've just gotten started. What about jealous wives?"

"Or a jealous older sister. Back to the big font. Great big font. Let's see." I resumed typing. *Cordelia lied about never being in Port Aransas before. She lied about the police finding the photo album. She kept us out of Bianca's bedroom. What did she think we'd find there?*

"By the way," I said. "I think we can rule out John. If he was going to kill anyone, it would be Cordelia."

"Good thinking.

Next, I typed, *Thelma Bigelow is a low-down, vicious, spiteful, rotten, mean-spirited witch.*

"I'm sure you're right. But what's left without all those adjectives?"

"That sounds very English-teacher-like. Can I—may I—keep the noun?"

"Sure. We'll stipulate she's a witch. What else?"

She got into a heated fight with Bianca, so we know she's not afraid to get physical.

"Now we're getting somewhere," Ryan said. "Still, it's a stretch between hair-pulling and stabbing."

"Who's the lawyer here?"

Ryan grinned and squeezed my shoulder, then got up and stretched before sitting down again. "Guess all your devil's-advocacy skills are rubbing off on me. Keep going."

"Medium-sized font for Ornella Hewett." *Used to badmouth Bianca, according to Doris, but put on a different face at Mayra's.*

"What about the manicurists?"

"I never even met Helen. As for Marlene, well, she's pretty handy with those pointy objects she works with. Bianca even said she'd stabbed her—or poked her, or something—with one of those implements, claiming it was an accident. But I think Marlene simply gets agitated easily. I don't think she'd really stab someone on purpose."

"I take it you like her too."

"I do."

"So I guess we can rule out all the people you like."

"You've out-deviled me. Well, at least we've established that lots of people have motives. If nothing else—if it comes to that—'reasonable doubt' should clear Miguel. But I'd rather see him cleared with NO doubt at all."

Chapter 26

I caught up with Lydia Wilson on my way to Mayra's the next morning, and we continued walking together.

"How's your nephew doing?" The kindness in her eyes almost brought tears to mine.

"Okay, I guess. Alana is torn between wanting to call him five times a day and not wanting to bug him. I left a message on his voicemail a couple of days ago, but haven't heard back."

"Well, I guess no news is good news." She blushed. "That sounds rather trite."

I smiled. "No, it sounds encouraging. I try to think of it that way."

She hesitated before speaking again. "If Thelma shows up—which she probably will—don't let anything she says get under your skin. None of the rest of us feel that way."

So. They had discussed it after I'd left—which I'd suspected would happen.

"I appreciate that—especially since I'm kind of a newcomer."

She laughed. "Up till you came, *I* was the new kid on the block."

"Really? I just figured everyone else had lived here forever."

"Not us. We used to come to the Island on vacation, but hadn't thought of moving here till we discovered these cottages had been renovated. They were—well—kinda dreary up till Roque bought them. He spent all summer before last fixing them up. Your nephews used to come down and help him. Nice kids."

"Gosh, I'd forgotten. Ryan and I were busy with our class reunions while that was going on."

"It was quite a project. Tom was ready to retire from the Navy, and we'd been looking for a place to settle down. Once the cottages were finished, we knew we'd found it."

The Wilsons were the only tenants with a yearly lease. Different families rented the other cottages, for a few days, or weeks, or however long their vacations lasted. People were friendly, but also wrapped up in their own holiday plans. The only neighbor I saw regularly, besides Lydia, was a young mother who took her baby for walks in his stroller. She'd stop if we were outside and admire our bougainvillea while we admired her baby.

"What about the folks who live in the mobile-home park?" I asked. "Have they always lived there? Doris and Fina and Gloria? Ornella? Even dear Thelma?"

"Hmm. They've lived there ever since it was built— maybe seven or eight years ago. Before that, I don't know."

By now we'd reached Mayra's and were greeted with the aroma of fresh-brewed coffee and cinnamon rolls. Mayra seemed a little guarded, or maybe I was projecting my own shift in perceptions. I wished I could erase some of Cordelia's remarks, some of my own observations. But most of all, it was a couple of Ryan's comments that gnawed at me. For one, if he was right that I refused to suspect people I liked, maybe I should make an effort to look at everyone differently.

Even Lydia. Ryan liked her husband. And Ryan was a pretty good judge of character. *Don't get sidetracked, Sharon. Ryan could be wrong too. Think.* Okay, Lydia and Tom were in their fifties at best, so must have retired early.

If someone as old and feeble as Mr. Edwards—the octogenarian we'd met a Mayra's luau so long ago—could be smitten with Bianca, why not someone still virile and active? Could Lydia's Tom have been involved with Bianca? Could Lydia have found out?

And if Dan Borrego really did have an affair—or even a one-night stand—with Bianca, Fina was too classy to make a public scene. If she discussed it with anyone at all, it would probably be with Gloria. And how easy would it be for Gloria to mislead her husband with phony "observations"? How much did Sgt. Bullis *really* tell her about the case?

Who else? I hadn't gotten to know all the women who came and went at Mayra's. Did all of them have philandering husbands?

Yeah, right. Every last one. I stifled a giggle.

"Something funny?" Thelma asked with a sneer. "Why don't you let us all in on it."

Everyone looked at me, and I felt my face flame.

"I'm just preoccupied—not very good company, I'm afraid. I'd hoped coming here would change that."

Fina reached across the table and placed her hand on mine. "You don't have to explain—anything."

Ryan was right. People I like are automatically innocent.

* * *

After the others left, I helped Mayra tidy up the kitchen, then sat at the table again. She sat opposite me, rather reluctantly it seemed. But I needed to ask her about the other issue that was bothering me.

"Mayra, I know you see a side to this that I don't, but I feel like I'm clawing my way through gauze. No one—well, no one except Thelma—points the finger at Miguel. But no one offers any other possibilities. No one seems alarmed that a dangerous killer might still be roaming the streets."

Mayra's shoulders sagged, and for a few moments she seemed old and tired, unlike her usual ebullient self. She got up, then poured us each another cup of coffee before seating herself again. "Whoever killed Bianca isn't a danger to anyone else," she said at last.

I blinked. "How can you be so sure? I mean, couldn't it be some psychopath? Maybe a serial killer?

She stared at me. "Do you believe that?"

I sighed. "No."

"Whoever it is, it's not a serial killer. Whoever killed Bianca did it because she provoked him."

"Or her."

"Hmph. Right. Or her."

"In other words, she asked for it."

"I'm not saying she deserved it. There's a difference."

"You're right. But doesn't anyone care if it just gets swept under the rug?"

Mayra studied her coffee cup a few moments. "The sad thing, Sharon, is that we've begun to believe it must be one of us, someone in our little community, and I don't think anyone feels a burning need to find out who. Too many people have too many secrets."

I suddenly felt sick, as if I'd turned Mayra's friendly kaffee klatch into a hub of suspicion and distrust. "Mayra, I'm sorry I put you on the spot. Asking you to help me clear Miguel."

"Oh no, dear." She patted my hand. "I want to help Miguel. None of this upheaval is your fault. Not at all. And certainly not Miguel's. It was Miss Bianca who set everything in motion."

Of course. Bianca's murder would have caused a swirl of questions and doubts with or without my interference.

Another question came to mind. "When you said 'too many secrets,' what did you mean?"

Mayra took a sip of coffee. "Slim's involvement with Bianca wasn't much of a secret. He and Thelma aren't very well liked, so that might be an 'easy' solution. One thing, Thelma's worried sick—but maybe it's because Slim *is* an obvious suspect. Maybe she's simply afraid he'll be falsely accused."

"Same as Miguel, " I murmured.

"But we like Miguel. We don't like Slim."

Ouch. There goes my faulty innocence/guilt detector again.

Mayra had sidestepped my question, but I gave it another try. "What other secrets?"

She didn't answer.

"You suspect someone, don't you."

"I don't think she meant to."

She? Mayra had spoken so softly I wasn't sure I'd heard correctly.

"Who?" I asked, equally softly.

Mayra clamped her lips together, and looked down at her hands.

I put my cup down, came around the table, and put my arm around her shoulders. "Forget I asked."

She stood and hugged me, tears in her eyes. "It shouldn't have happened," she whispered.

Chapter 27

It really didn't matter what Mayra or I suspected, or what secrets anyone was hiding. What mattered was the police investigation, which, as best I could tell, wasn't going anywhere.

Or so I thought. I reached the footpath between the dunes and the picket fence that ran behind all the cottages and continued walking home. Before I got very far, I saw the path cordoned off behind our place and the cottages on either side. When I got as close as I could, I found Sgts. Fay and Bullis outside our back gate while another cop appeared to be digging a shallow trench along the edge of the picket fence.

"What's going on?" I asked.

"Would you mind waiting inside?" Sgt. Fay asked politely.

Yes, I would mind. But I turned around and went to the end of the block, then hurried down the sidewalk in front of our cottages till I got home.

"What's going on?" I repeated to Ryan when I came inside.

He turned away from the kitchen window, where he was keeping watch. "I don't know. I went back and asked the same thing, but they weren't very informative."

Although I told myself that whatever they were looking for couldn't have anything to do with us—or with Miguel—I still felt squeamish. I joined Ryan by the window and slipped my hand into his, hoping it would calm my increasing anxiety.

The digging stopped. One of the men bent down. When he rose, he was holding a long slim object. A knife? Hard to tell from a distance. He slipped it—whatever it was—into a small bag.

The three cops consulted among themselves, then came through the gate and knocked at our back door. When we answered, Sgt. Bullis said, "Ms. Salazar, would you come with us to the station to talk with Lt. Richmond?"

And what if I say no? "Sure. May I take my own car?"

"Sure. We'll follow," Sgt. Fay said pleasantly.

As if no one would notice that either.

Sgts. Bullis and Fay headed for their car, which they'd parked at the end of the street, while the other cop walked with Ryan and me to the carport and waited for his ride to pull up in front of our house.

"Want me to drive?" Ryan asked.

"No." After we buckled up, I explained. "Driving'll help me settle down."

I backed out, then made a point of going below the speed limit all the way into town. I waved at my young neighbor, who was walking her baby and giving us a puzzled look.

My uneasiness was giving way to a slow-burning anger, which caused me to think of various smart-aleck remarks I'd do better keeping to myself. Instead, I vented to Ryan.

"Why am I singled out? Why don't they want to talk to you?"

"Beats me. But better you than Miguel."

We were quiet the rest of the way, while I mulled over what my interview could possibly mean.

After we arrived at the station, the officers deposited Ryan in the reception area, their find on Lt. Richmond's desk, and me in the chair across from him. After the paperwork was done, they left, closing the door behind them and leaving Lt. Richmond and me to stare at each other.

"Thank you for coming in," he said.

"My pleasure." I bit my lip.

I accepted his offer of something cold to drink and opted for water rather than soda. Then he turned on the recorder, and we went through the standard preliminaries.

"Do you know why you're here?" he began.

"No. I guess it has something to do with those men digging behind our house."

"They found a weapon that appears to have been used in Bertha Lumpkin's murder."

"Hmm. They seemed to know exactly where to look. And at such a late date too. I'm guessing they got an anonymous so-called tip?"

"So far, so good."

"This person who provided the tip—man or woman?"

"Couldn't really tell."

"What specifically did they say?"

"That they'd seen you bury the murder weapon."

"*Me*?"

"Shortly after Ms. Lumpkin's murder."

"Why did they wait so long to report this?"

"Said they were afraid."

I rolled my eyes.

He leaned back and linked his hands behind his head. "And the implication was that either your nephew had stabbed Ms. Lumpkin and you were covering for him, or you'd stabbed her yourself."

"Good grief. Well, here's my theory. The person who called you planted the knife, or whatever it was." I raised my hand. "I know. That's what they all say, but listen a minute."

Lt. Richmond waited and, to my surprise, did listen without interrupting.

"First of all, Bianca was murdered nearly a week ago. That would give someone—me included—plenty of time to get rid of the murder weapon, which, incidentally, I'm not convinced is that object on your desk."

He folded his arms across his chest and continued listening.

"Now. If it were mine—say it's a knife—I might hide it for a day or two, then I'd toss it in someone else's trash container—preferably our neighbor's with all the dirty diapers. Or maybe in one of the containers along the beach. The trash would be picked up Monday, and that would be that."

"What about your nephew? Maybe that's who the informant saw. Maybe Ms. Lumpkin's death was an accident. Mr. Meléndez panicked, hid the weapon in the first place that came to mind...."

I shook my head. "There are too many holes in that picture. Here's my "maybe." Maybe someone assumed you'd think the stabbing took place in front of our house, so hiding the knife nearby would be logical. But we both know Bianca was killed someplace else, then left in our yard."

He raised his eyebrows. "Oh? What makes you so sure?"

"Because—"

Because if Leo could figure it out, so could you.

I shuddered. "Because of all the blood."

"You saw the body?"

"Briefly, but the image is still there in my mind." I closed my eyes a moment, trying to push away the memory. I took a few swallows of water, the ice-cold liquid slowing the motion of my stomach if not my nerves. "When my brother-in-law found her, he said the way the blood was smeared, it made him think she'd been dragged there." The words seemed awkward, unfeeling—but it was the only way I could get them out.

"Supposing you're right. She could have been killed about midnight and left at your place later—about the time you heard the dog bark. By the way, we checked on that with your neighbors. They heard the dog and let him inside, but they didn't hear any car."

I barely heard his last remarks, stuck on his theory that Bianca could have been killed around midnight. Was that what the post mortem showed? Could Bianca have been killed while Miguel was still in Port Aransas? I couldn't prove the car I heard had anything to do with her death. Miguel couldn't prove his timetable.

Forget the bogus weapon. Miguel was still a suspect.

Chapter 28

"Okay," I said slowly, "supposing we're both right."

"Looking at both sides again."

"I try. For starters, do you know where she might have been killed?"

"No."

I didn't know if he was telling the truth or not but plowed ahead. "Let's say it was someplace the killer didn't want the body found. If I had done it—remember, this is just a big 'if'—why not move her to the dunes, or an abandoned building, or something?" I perked up. "That's the big fallacy in suspecting either my nephew or me. Why on earth would either of us have moved her to our front yard?"

"You tell me."

"We wouldn't have. But someone else might, for the very purpose of incriminating Miguel."

"Then why your yard and not his?"

"Because...they got the cottages mixed up."

His eyes lit up, like a teacher whose backward student finally gets the right answer. "Maybe."

"Of course. Ours is the fourth one on one end of the block, and the Meléndezes is the fourth counting from the other end."

"So all we need to do is find someone who's dyslexic."

"That should narrow it down."

"Suppose someone did plant that weapon. Any ideas who it might be?"

"To tell you the truth, I can't imagine *anyone* crouching along the footpath without being seen. Of course, you're not likely to run into many joggers at night, but still, you never know who might be looking out the window."

"True. But someone could go very late, make sure all the lights were out, figure everyone has gone to bed, and jog along the path till they got behind your place."

"Wouldn't the digging make noise?"

"Not necessarily. It wasn't deep."

"Well, this time, I don't think it was the dyslexic person. I think it was someone who knew exactly what she was doing."

"She?"

"Off the record?"

Lt. Richmond turned off the recorder.

"This is just a guess, but I can think of only one person who dislikes me enough to do something like that."

"Name?"

I hesitated. "Thelma Bigelow."

"Any particular reason? Besides not liking you?"

"I think she suspects her own husband."

"Ah yes. His name has come up."

That surprised me. I hadn't thought they were really looking beyond Miguel.

"You know what," I said. "I'm beginning to wonder.... Either Thelma thinks the police are stupid—sorry about that—or she's secretly hoping Slim will get caught while she 'stands by her man.'"

"What makes you think that?"

"Well, she's made a big production of making Miguel look bad, and all it's done is turn attention to Slim. So, if that's her plan, maybe she buried the right knife after all!"

"We'll check it out, of course. But by itself, it doesn't lead anywhere."

"Especially if it turns out to be phony."

"So we're back to that." Lt. Richmond shook his head. "I didn't really get you here on false pretenses, but I like listening to the way that mind of yours works. I can question Ms. Bigelow, but I don't have much to go on."

"No, I'd let it go. You might focus on Slim instead. Bianca's car was actually his, registered in his name. And they were supposedly having an affair."

"So go the rumors."

Evidently Lt. Richmond wasn't going to fill me in on his conversation with Slim, if any.

"Oh, just remembered—did you have a chance to talk to Cordelia before she left?"

It was a day for eye-rolling.

"Caught her and John at the airport. Poor guy. I'd hate to have to—Never mind."

"Did they say anything helpful?"

He shrugged. "Don't know yet. By the way, did your nephew ever mention a Charley Borrego?"

"No-o-o. Old boyfriend of Bianca's?"

"According to the sister."

"How convenient! Maybe Cordelia's just tossing names to the wind to divert attention from herself."

"Yeah. Well." Lt. Richmond stood. "I've kept you long enough."

I stood too. "Maybe some of the kaffee klatchers saw me come down here after all. Might be a good thing. Unearth some fascinating guesswork. Maybe even something helpful."

He smiled and saluted me.

Chapter 29

Lt. Richmond walked me to the reception area, where I introduced him to Ryan.

"I was glad to see that look of relief on your face," Ryan remarked after we left the station. "Guess they're saving the rack for another time."

I laughed. "I was glad to see you two shake hands."

We waited till we got home and were settled on the sofa with Ryan's Tecate and my Dr. Pepper in hand before I related the interview in detail.*

"At least Miguel isn't the *only* suspect anymore," I said. "But I bet they haven't written him off completely. I think Lt. Richmond follows my logic, but we all know people do illogical things."

"Good to hear they're considering other people—Slim, Cordelia."

"Almost forgot, Cordelia told Lt. Richmond about someone named Charley Borrego. This must be the same person she mentioned to me when she was listing Bianca's conquests. Charley, not Dan, thank goodness.

"Questioning all her conquests should keep them busy."

"There's something else nagging at me. Both Mayra and Lt. Richmond said things that indicated the stabbing might not have been intentional."

"How can you stab someone three or four times without it being intentional?"

"I don't know. When Lt. Richmond suggested it could have been an accident, I thought it was just a trick question. Giving me a chance to admit I knew about it. But then I put his comment together with what Mayra said earlier today when we were talking about who could have killed Bianca. I don't remember the exact words, but it was something like, 'Maybe she didn't mean to.'"

"She?"

"I'm not positive. Whichever—he or she—I remember Leo said the stabbing didn't make sense. That the wounds were inconsistent. Maybe it was even self-defense."

"That's a stretch."

I pushed stubbornly ahead. "Why? Why not self-defense? And if it was a woman, what if she got some cuts herself and covered them up? Ornella Hewett always wears long-sleeved blouses, no matter how warm it is."

"Sharon, maybe the woman likes long-sleeved blouses."

I sighed. "Go ahead. Insert a little common sense. See if I care."

Ryan leaned over and kissed me on the cheek.

I made a face, then smiled at him. "Okay. So there could be a good explanation. And I'm not running this by anyone else. But something—strange. Lt. Richmond ended the interview rather abruptly after I suggested Cordelia was throwing names around. It bothers me that he might think I was doing the same thing by accusing Thelma."

"I doubt he thinks that. You probably just gave him some idea he wanted to follow up on."

"Anyway, I'm not about to throw any more names his way without something to back them up."

"Good idea. No need to borrow trouble."

*   *   *

I'm not always sure where to draw the line between borrowing trouble and being prepared. I don't like being caught off-guard. Still, following Ryan's advice, I told myself

I should just let the police do their jobs and mind my own business.

I didn't have much chance to do otherwise. Ryan and I returned to San Antonio the next day—a week to the day since Bianca's murder. It seemed we'd been gone longer than that, and we were both glad to be home again. We puttered around the house the rest of Saturday, went to church and relaxed on Sunday, and began our workweek Monday.

Miguel was back in San Antonio, after having gone to Zapata for the weekend, so we asked him and Leo to come over for lasagna Monday night. I was dismayed to find Miguel looking thin and drawn, with dark circles under his eyes. We kept the conversation light, and he made an effort to join in.

Ryan and Leo had cooked, so Miguel and I were on k.p. after dinner. At first we worked in silence, Miguel loading the dishwasher while I wiped off the stove and counters.

Then he said, "It's more awkward to avoid talking about Bianca than to talk about her."

"I think we needed to hear that from you. C'mon, let's take a break. We can finish this later."

He nodded and we went out on the porch and sat on the glider. After a few moments, he reached over and squeezed my hand, then released it, stood up and began pacing back and forth.

"At first it was so—surreal, I guess that's the word. Now I feel like I'm on a see-saw. I was angry with her. Then I felt sorry for her. Then I was angry they thought I was guilty. Now I just feel like I'm—" He spread out his arms, then dropped them to his sides and sat down again—"in outer space somewhere. I keep waiting for them to knock on my door and ask more questions or something."

145

"If it's any comfort, they've been questioning other people too. By the way, does the name Charley Borrego mean anything to you?"

"Charley? Yeah. Why?"

"I take it he was an old boyfriend of Bianca's."

"Used to be a friend of mine. Kind of."

"Really? Tell me."

"Last year when Gabe and I came down to help Tío Roque, Charley was on the construction crew. We got to be buddies."

"And Bianca wasn't on the scene yet?"

"Right. She got here last winter sometime—January? Maybe February. I don't know exactly when she started going out with Charley."

"And when you came down in June, she dropped Charley?"

Miguel's face reddened. "I wouldn't have even known if she hadn't told me. She said he was real jealous, and she hoped he wouldn't do something to get even."

"Uh-oh. Was there trouble?"

"Nope. Not really. But there was one thing. We'd gone to one of those stupid concerts. Bianca said she was cold, and I went back to the Jeep to get her sweater. So on the way, Charley comes up to me and says, 'If you know what's good for you, you'll stay away from her.' So I tell him to back off, that she can make up her own mind. He just looks at me and calls me an idiot and walks off."

"You remember it that clearly?"

"Yeah. That's because I've played it over in my mind since then. At first, I thought he meant it as a threat against me. Now, I think he was warning me about her."

"Good ol' hindsight. That does make more sense. Especially since he just dropped it."

146

"He's not a suspect, is he?"

"I don't think so. They might question him, but...."

Miguel shook his head. "Charley wouldn't kill her. He wouldn't have any reason to."

So. I wasn't the only one to consider my friends innocent.

"Do you know if he's related to Dan and Fina Borrego?" I asked.

"Could be. Maybe a nephew or something. All I know, his mom's name is Viola. They have a big family too."

Fina had always been so sympathetic. Now I wondered if it was because *her* nephew had been involved with Bianca too. If Ryan were here, he'd say he could see the wheels turning in my head.

Chapter 30

I talked Ryan into going to the Island again the following weekend so I could—as he put it—engage in my busybody tactics.

It was now November, two weeks since Bianca's death. The weather had turned chilly and cloudy, and my hooded turquoise sweatsuit kept me warm as I took the footpath over to Mayra's Saturday morning.

The usual crowd had gathered, but I noticed that the previous hot topic of conversation—Bianca's murder—wasn't even alluded to. Was this because they'd simply exhausted the subject, or was it because, as Mayra had suggested, they were afraid of unearthing family skeletons.

This week, it was Fina who seemed a little remote. I decided to stop in at their computer shop later and see if I could eke out some information. When I arrived at the front desk early that afternoon, I was glad to find Fina alone. She seemed surprised to see me, not unfriendly, but somewhat wary. Business was slow, she told me, and her daughter Valerie was taking a long break. Dan was busy with repairs in the back.

"Fina, I need to talk to you. In private, if we can."

"We can talk here," she said reluctantly. "If it gets busy, we can continue somewhere else when Valerie gets back."

I took a deep breath. "I have questions about a Charley Borrego. Is he a relative of yours?"

Her eyes narrowed. "Yes."

I waited.

"He's the son of one of Dan's second cousins," she said at last, looking past me to a picture on the wall. "And yes, he's been questioned by Lt. Richmond."

"Oh! Well, I knew they'd widened the investigation."

"*Someone* suggested they look at Charley."

"Do you think I'm the one who did that?"

"The idea occurred to me."

"Oh dear. You think we were looking for a scapegoat? Believe me, I didn't even know about Charley till Lt. Richmond asked me if Miguel knew him. So—when we went home—I asked Miguel. He said no way would Charley be guilty."

Fina looked at me then, doubtful, but less defensive.

"I was surprised you'd never mentioned Charley's involvement with Bianca," I continued. "You know, to kind of commiserate with me."

"Well, I did commiserate. But I wasn't about to bring up Charley's name—especially in front of the whole group."

"You could've called."

The front door opened, accompanied by a loud jingle, and in walked Valerie. She greeted me cheerfully, then gave Fina a quizzical look after seeing her guarded expression.

Fina smiled, then asked her daughter to mind the shop while we took a break.

"'K. Don't hurry."

Fina donned a coat and scarf, and we walked to a nearby park, which was surprisingly busy, considering the gloomy day.

"Let's go to my house," I suggested. "Ryan's gone for the day—went down to Corpus to see an old college friend."

After we were seated at the kitchen table, each with a cup of hot chocolate, Fina looked around the room approvingly. "I like the sunflowers in your curtains," she said. "Yellow is a cheerful color—the way a kitchen should be."

I hoped that meant we'd broken through the ice. But maybe not.

"What else do you want to know about Charley?" Her tone was flat.

"I wondered if he and Bianca had broken up because of Miguel."

"Bianca." She said the name with contempt. "No. It was much worse."

She stirred her hot chocolate, blending the melting marshmallows into the steaming liquid.

"No," she continued, "I wasn't aware of what was going on with Charley back then—I'm doing well to keep track of my own kids. It wasn't till things got ugly that I found out any of it."

"I can relate to that. And I can see why you didn't want it brought up at Mayra's."

"I'm glad you understand. And probably most of the others would too—with one notable exception." She paused. "I'm trusting you to keep this to yourself. I don't know how many people know outside our family, but it's something we'd just as soon not advertise. You see, Charley wasn't 'in love with' Bianca. He just went out with her 'for fun.' Some fun, as it turned out. Anyway, maybe because he's older than Miguel, he wised up faster."

"So he was the one who broke it off?"

"Oh, yes. Bianca didn't take kindly to being dumped."

"So Miguel discovered."

"I don't know what threats she used with Miguel, but she told Charley she was pregnant."

My eyes widened. Apparently Bianca's *modus operandi*.

"*Then* she proceeded to tell him she wanted $10,000 for an abortion."

"My god! Was she hoping to haggle for a better price?"

"Possibly. Charley threw a dent in her scheme by telling her he didn't believe in abortion, and he'd pay child support instead—IF the baby turned out to be his."

"I can just imagine her reaction to that."

"She threatened then to tell the police he'd raped her. He told her they'd probably do some tests. I don't know if they would. I don't know if Charley knew either, but she went back to extorting money. She hit up Charley's dad, then Dan, which is the only way I'd have ever known. Dan told her to go to hell. I guess she figured she'd keep trying till she found someone who'd believe her. She really was delusional."

"What made her give up?"

"She tried to get it from another uncle. Big mistake on her part. Ramon told her he'd taped their conversation and was taking it straight to the police."

"Had he? Taped it, I mean."

"I don't know. What I do know is she stalked off and left Charley alone after that."

"She tried to make Miguel think Charley would be jealous."

"Oh, like *that* would happen. I'm guessing Charley was glad when she snared someone else." Fina stopped. "That was tactless. Not glad it was Miguel."

"You're right. They were friends—or used to be. He even tried to warn Miguel, but Miguel wasn't listening."

"Well, now that the cops are looking at other 'suspects'—including Charley, unfortunately—I hope that means Miguel is off the list."

"I wish. I doubt if he's off completely, but maybe he's slipped down a notch or two. Let's hope he and Charley are at the bottom of *that* heap."

Fina smiled. "I'm glad you and I are on the same side. I'd come to think of you as a friend, and it bothered me that—well, you know."

"I do know. I feel the same way."

"I suppose I should get back to the shop," she said with a sigh.

"Oh, play hooky a while longer. Valerie seemed to have things well in hand. Besides, I just thought of something else I'd like to run by you."

Chapter 31

"I guess you could bribe me with more hot chocolate," Fina said.

I laughed and poured us more cocoa with plenty of marshmallows to mush into the brew.

"Tell me about your kids," I said. "I feel like I've known you forever, but there's so much I don't know at all."

"Don't get me started! That's my favorite subject."

We chatted amiably for a while, till Fina reminded me that I'd wanted to bring up something else.

"You got me thinking," I said. "Here I've always thought Bianca was just out to seduce as many men as she could. But what if her real motive is extortion?"

"You mean other people besides Charley?"

"Exactly. But with different threats." I didn't want to bring up Marlene's or Mayra's names, but things they'd said began coming together. "What if some guy didn't want his wife to find out, and Bianca held that over his head. Or what if she had something on Slim, for example. I don't know. Maybe she found out something illegal going on at his dealership."

"You might have something. Oh, wow. The possibilities are endless. From working at the office, she knew just about everyone in Vista Sonrisa. She probably overheard a lot—picked up things she could nail people with."

"Besides that, everyone's names must be in the office files."

"True. But I doubt there's anything unusual in those. Private, maybe. Like late payments or something. Not anything you'd let yourself get blackmailed about."

"More likely, just as you said. She heard something on the office grapevine and hit paydirt." I shook my head. "I've met so many people through Mayra—either at her luau ages ago or over coffee—and it's hard to imagine any of them harboring nasty secrets."

"'Only the shadow knows.' Or...it could be my sister-in-law's sister-in-law's neighbor. I don't know her real name. We all call her 'Hyacinth'—you know, after the character on that British TV comedy. She likes to tell everyone that her only son has a very lucrative career and lives in a gated community."

"I take it he doesn't?"

"He had a lucrative career, all right, robbing banks. His gated community is down in Huntsville."

This started us both laughing.

"What about Thelma?" I said. "Maybe she has a sinister secret. She strikes me as a Nazi sympathizer."

"Ha. Wouldn't surprise me if she was a member of the Gestapo. But I don't think she'd mind anyone knowing. Oh, I shouldn't be so hard on her. She hasn't always been so disagreeable."

"Really? This is something recent?"

"She's always been a little, what would you call it? Grim? But not so confrontational. I think she's worried about Slim. No one says so out loud, but he's bound to be an obvious suspect too."

So maybe Thelma isn't *trying to set him up.*

Neither of us suggested other possible blackmail victims. I knew it would be hard for Fina to consider people who'd been friends for who-knows-how-many years. I suspected we had similar innocence/guilt criteria. So we slid into more comfortable subjects until Fina said she *really* had to get back to the shop.

*   *   *

Although it was after 4:00 when I dropped Fina off, I drove to Tío Roque's office, hoping he'd be there instead of in the field, as he so often was. On the way I called Ryan, who said he'd just started home. I told him to meet me at Tío's instead. He could return Tío's car, and maybe we could all go out to dinner later.

When I reached the office, I knocked lightly on the door and opened it a crack.

"Tío? Are you there?"

Hearing my voice, he boomed out, "Come in, mijita. Don't stand outside in the cold!"

He was already on his way to the door, and greeted me with a bear hug.

"Come in, come in. John and I were just sitting here shooting the breeze."

"Oh, you have company?"

"No, not 'company.' You and John aren't company. Can I get you something to drink?"

"No, thanks, I'm hot-chocolated out." I smiled at John, then sat in one of the navy-blue armchairs facing the coffee table. "Hope I'm not interrupting."

"Not at all. I should be going soon anyway," John said, half-rising.

"Please don't leave on my account, or I'll feel guilty."

"Well, I wouldn't want you to do that." John gave me a tired smile and sank back into a matching armchair, while Tío Roque went to the kitchen to replenish their drinks.

John looked haggard, the strain of the past weeks telling on him. I found myself suddenly tongue-tied. The last time

I'd seen him, we'd skirted around any direct mention of Bianca's death. Now, here at Tío Roque's, we didn't have any busywork or Cordelia's hostility to distract us. Here we faced each other: the uncle of the murder victim and the aunt of the prime suspect. But, as with Miguel, it seemed as uncomfortable to ignore Bianca as to acknowledge her. I took a chance.

"John, I hope it's not too late to offer my sympathy."

He closed his eyes and rubbed his forehead. "Thanks. It's been hard. Bertha was sort of mixed up, but I always thought she'd come around."

Tío Roque returned with mugs of Tecate. "You sure you don't want anything?" he asked me again.

"Positive. Now what were you two discussing before I barged in?"

"Oh, that," Tío said with a wave of his arm as he sat down, then took a few swallows of beer. "Tourists."

"The Winter Texans have begun trickling in," John said.

"Can't live without 'em. I've already rented one of the cottages to a retired couple for the whole season. So you'll have new neighbors soon."

"Just think how rich you'd be if your relatives didn't take up so much space!" I said.

He waved that suggestion away too. "I have everything I need. Including my family. *Especially* my family."

"You're lucky," John said somberly. "The farther I am from what's left of my relatives, the better."

No wonder. Cordelia. Her bigoted parents.... Not exactly a Norman Rockwell gathering.

Tío and I exchanged uncomfortable glances, no doubt wishing the conversation hadn't veered in that direction.

"Um, if the new neighbors are coming down to escape the cold, I hope this weather isn't scaring them," I said. *Surely weather's a safe topic.*

Tío Roque smiled. "Oh, they think it's balmy here compared to Minnesota."

John set what was left of his beer on the coffee table, then rose, saying he needed to be on his way. I was relieved, to tell you the truth, worried that I might bring up another touchy subject. Besides, I wanted to talk with Tío one-on-one. I thought he might be more willing to list Bianca's enemies—and be more objective—than Fina had been.

Chapter 32

"I didn't expect John to take this so hard," I said after he'd left and Tío and I were sitting comfortably in the plump navy chairs again. "I didn't think he and Bianca got along that well."

"Oh, it's what people feel sometimes—wishing they could have patched things up before it was too late. Hasn't changed Cordelia a bit. She's mean as ever."

"Cordelia! Has she shown up again?"

"Not a chance. But shortly after she left town, they released Bianca's body, and there was a big quarrel about that. John got "second-hand hell" over the phone. None of her family wanted to take her back to Louisiana. Cordelia wanted her cremated and forgotten. John thought she deserved some dignity and saw to it she had a memorial service."

"When was this?"

"The service? Couple of days ago."

"I wonder if Miguel knew about it."

"I doubt it. It was pretty short notice. Nothing in the paper."

"Just as well. Miguel has enough to deal with."

"True."

"Did anyone...um, how many people showed up?"

"Not too many. People from the mobile-home park who wanted to pay John their respects."

"I suppose the police came?"

"Yeah, the Bullises were there. I guess that's what cops do. If anyone was acting strange, it sure went by me."

"Were Thelma and Slim there?"

Tío Roque peered at me over his thick glasses, his eyes twinkling. "You want a list?"

I smiled back. "Sure. But you said it would be a short one. Just the people we both know."

"Okay, the Hewetts and the Wilsons were there. Let's see. Doris. Mayra and me, o'course. And to answer your question, no, the Bigelows weren't there, Neither were any of the Borregos. That's probably because the cops had picked up Charley Borrego earlier."

Word does get around. "How come?"

"Ex-boyfriend. Long time ago. Don't know why they'd bother him now. Charlie has a temper, but I can't see him killing anyone."

Temper? Fina didn't mention that. "Miguel said he used to work for you."

"Good worker. I like Charley."

We were each quiet a few minutes, mulling over our own thoughts.

"Let me know if you change your mind about something to drink," Tío offered again."

"I'll take you up on that. I am getting thirsty. Water'll be fine."

I followed Tío out to the kitchen, which was really just a small alcove with a fridge, microwave, hotplate, and coffeepot, plus a cabinet with cups, mismatched mugs, plates, glasses, and a variety of "instant" goodies: coffee, cocoa, creamer, real and fake sugar.

After pouring me a glass of water and himself another Tecate, we moved back to the reception area, which seemed to me to have all the amenities of a homey living room.

Besides the coffee table and easy chairs, there were end tables with lamps and magazines, and a television—complete with DVD player. On the light blue walls were several peaceful seascapes, many of them painted by Alana. I wondered if he spent more time here than at his own home, which was one-half of a small duplex not far from his rental cottages.

"You got called in too, I hear," Tío said with a crooked grin.

"Oh, yeah." I gave him an abridged version of the knife incident.

"Huh!" he snorted. "Don't the cops have something better to do?"

"I'm sure they'd rather. Obviously, they haven't found the real murder weapon, and apparently don't have any evidence to link *anyone* to Bianca's death. Yet."

"So till then, Miguel's got this...dark cloud...hanging over his head."

"That's what bothers me. The thing is, I'm convinced Bianca was blackmailing any number of people."

Tío's eyebrows shot up, and he stroked his mustache. "I wouldn't put it past her."

"So that would give a lot of people motives."

"Well, if it occurred to you, I bet the cops have thought of it too."

"Could be."

"Then I'll be first in line when they start asking questions."

"You are joking, aren't you?"

"'Fraid not."

I sank back in my chair, not knowing what else to say.

"I used to have a guy working for me—Manny Atencio. One of the hardest workers I'd ever known. Dependable. We were trying to get him a green card, but those things can take time."

"And Bianca found out."

"Probably through Charley. It was back when she was going with him, so I guess he mentioned it, without knowing what she was like. After they broke up, that's when she threatened to turn us in."

"Did she threaten you, or Charley?"

"Me. She must've thought I had big bucks. I didn't pay her anything. I knew if it started, it would never stop."

"So what did you do?"

"I wanted to find another place for Manny to work, but he disappeared. He was afraid of being deported. I was so mad when I realized he'd left, I went down to the office and reamed out Bianca in front of everyone."

"Who was there, besides John?"

"John was out. There were just a couple of women who'd come in to pay their rent. Doris Hood was the only one I knew."

"Doris?" *Down-to-earth Doris?* "So what did you say to Bianca that they overheard?"

"That I'd like to wring her neck. And I didn't just *say* it. I yelled it."

"Oh dear. Do you think those women would tell the cops?"

"Not Doris. Don't know about the other one. But not Doris."

Score another point for friends' innocence.

"Well, the good news is, you've proved my point that Bianca was into blackmail. And she might have hit up someone who did more than yell. I'd like to pick your brain for things you might have heard—or seen, or noticed—that'll help us figure it out."

161

"That's the job for the police, mijita."

"I know. But no matter how much questioning they do, people say things to each other they don't say to cops."

Tío Roque thought that over. "Okay. I know of people Bianca might have gotten to. But I don't know anyone who'd have killed her."

"We're just brainstorming, Tío. This is just between the two of us."

A knock on the door told us Ryan was here.

"Just the three of us," I amended as Tío got up to let Ryan in. I joined them at the door so I could give Ryan a hug.

He kissed me lightly on the lips, then declined Tío's offer of a Tecate. "I'll wait. Sharon said we might all go out for dinner later."

Tío looked at the clock on his file cabinet. "Is it that time already?"

"Pretty soon. It's already starting to get dark," I said, then turned to Ryan. "Are you starving?"

"I'm not in a hurry. Roger and I had a late lunch."

Ryan took off his windbreaker and hung it on the coat rack. Then we all sat down again.

"Sharon's got some ideas that might help clear Miguel," Tío said.

"I haven't even had a chance to talk to you about it," I told Ryan. "But I'm sure Bianca had some blackmail scheme going. And we're trying to come up with names of possible victims."

Ryan seemed to withdraw. "What are you going to do with these names?"

"That's just what I wanted to know," Tío said.

Their attitude hurt my feelings. I scowled at Ryan. "What do you think? I'm going to run around blabbing false accusations all over town?"

"Calm down, honey. I don't think that at all. Tell me what you've come up with so far."

I suppose telling Fina's story would have given me more credibility, but I didn't want to break her confidence. Instead, I looked at Tío Roque, who shrugged, then repeated his story.

Ryan whistled. "A predator in more ways than one. That really widens the circle. So who's next on the list?"

Again I looked at Tío, who'd been about to say more before Ryan arrived.

Tío rubbed his mustache again. "Keith Hewett's wife."

"Ornella?"

"I know, mijita. It seems unlikely, But she was in a car accident about a year ago. Took some heavy-duty pain pills."

"I see. So she got dependent on the pills?"

"And then after they didn't work anymore, she went to the hard stuff."

"Heroin?"

"I think. Needle marks all over her arms. She looks like a skeleton."

"She hides it well. Except for her face." I remembered noticing how thin, almost emaciated, her face looked.

"And Keith is nervous as a cat most of the time."

I remembered that too.

"So that adds to your blackmail theory," Tío said with finality. "But that's all."

Chapter 33

We went out to dinner at Thaiphoon's. (I have a weakness for their grilled chicken in peanut sauce.) By mutual consent, we banned any further talk about Bianca, murder, blackmail, and other dark subjects.

Ryan was somewhat quiet at the restaurant and even quieter on the way home.

"What's on your mind?" I asked.

He gripped the steering wheel and stared straight ahead. "Not much." He hesitated. "I was just surprised when Roger brought up something about Bianca's murder."

"Really? What did he say?"

"Not much. Just started me thinking."

"What is it that's bothering you?" *Please don't say "Not much" again.*

"Honey, let's just drop it for now, okay?"

"Okay."

"I need to give it some more thought, okay?"

"Okay."

Ryan reached for my hand, linking our fingers together. He knew me too well. I'd have one question after another once we got started on whatever was gnawing at him. And I knew Ryan well enough to realize discussion time was over.

Still, I wondered if the questions already spinning in my mind would fly out of my head of their own accord. What had Roger said? What did he know about the murder, and why was he interested? Did he suspect someone? Did Ryan suspect someone?

When we got home, Ryan turned on the boob tube—another way of walling off conversation. I left him in the living room, set up my laptop in the kitchen, and pulled up the earlier questions Ryan and I had raised about potential suspects. I tacked my current questions onto this list.

While I was at it, I updated the list of names, adding or subtracting as seemed relevant. I crossed off Marlene and Helen and their husbands. After Mayra's comment—and maybe even before—it seemed more likely that the killer would be someone closer to home.

If female, I typed, *Ornella was too frail to have moved Bianca.*

But what about her husband? *Keith Hewett: Killer or co-conspirator?*

Thelma is certainly strong enough. She & Slim could alibi each other.

But Mayra doesn't like them. It doesn't seem she'd have been so distraught if they were guilty.

Could Mayra have been thinking of Lydia, or Fina, or Doris?

Of course, I didn't know every single woman in the neighborhood, the way Mayra probably did. And even if Mayra did suspect one of them, that wouldn't necessarily make it so.

Mayra's pronouns really weren't clear. Maybe I misunderstood. Maybe Mayra said "he" instead of "she."

Maybe she suspected Tío Roque. I couldn't believe she'd seriously consider him, and I refused to add his name to the roster. On the other hand, Mayra was very fond of him...in love with him? That could certainly account for her distress. And she probably knew about his illegal hiring.

I was giving myself a headache, so closed out the document and shut off the computer. I went back to the living room, snuggled up to Ryan, and laid my head on his shoulder. "I'm tired of thinking," I whispered. "Let's just make love."

He chuckled and drew me closer. "That beats thinking any time."

*   *   *

Sunday morning dawned sunny and warm—a welcome change from yesterday's dismal weather. After church and a leisurely breakfast, Ryan and I repaid Tío Roque by tending the garden in the back yard, alternately pulling weeds and stopping to enjoy the profusion of red, pink, and yellow hibiscus.

When I heard Lydia Wilson talking to Barky across the way, I stood, brushed flecks of dirt off my knees, and trotted over to speak to her.

She looked up and gave me a quick wave, then went back to attaching a leash to the little Yorkie's collar, while he wiggled and jumped up and down.

"One of us is taking the other for a walk if I can get him to hold still," she said. "Want to come with?"

"I'd love to. Give me a minute."

"Not to worry. Take a few."

I told Ryan I'd be back soon, dropped my gardening gloves on the patio, rinsed my hands off at the hydrant, and shook them dry on the way to the footpath.

I waited while Lydia finished securing Barky's leash. He was small but feisty, and could hardly wait to push through the gate to give me excited kisses. Then he tore off to do doggy things: sniff, pee, dash in circles. We walked past the dunes to the beach. Lydia kept a firm grip, but gave him a wide lead.

For several sun-warmed minutes, we watched Barky happily chase the laughing gulls before we continued our stroll. Except for a few gaily colored umbrellas that had popped up at random and a few surfboarders riding the waves, we had the beach to ourselves.

"Sharon," Lydia said, "I hope you don't mind my asking, but...what's been going on? I mean, all the digging and everything, and you, uh...."

"Going down to the police station?"

She blushed.

"It's okay," I said. "People are bound to be curious."

"Well, the police have come by, oh, a couple of times, asking Tom and me questions."

"I knew they'd asked if you'd seen anything the night Bianca was killed. But I didn't know they'd come by again."

"I'm afraid we weren't helpful...either time. We remembered bringing Barky inside that night. If they'd asked a few days later, we probably wouldn't have remembered at all. I mean, he goes in and out."

"You didn't notice something that might have set him off?"

"Not really. We figured it was a stray cat. He usually ignores them, but sometimes they come too close."

"And I guess you didn't hear a car."

Lydia shook her head. "We didn't even notice what time it was."

"No reason you should. It's the first time—well, the only time—Barky ever woke me up, so I was sort of alarmed."

"I'm glad to hear that. Not that you were alarmed, but that he's not a bother." She turned her attention to the dog. "Well, it looks like you've worn out all the gulls, Barky. Let's call it a day."

We turned around and ambled toward home.

"Lydia, what about the other time?"

She gave an involuntary jerk of Barky's leash. "What?"

"You said the police had questioned you twice."

"Oh."

Lydia tugged on the leash again, and Barky trotted to her side, somewhat subdued, as if sensing tension in her demeanor. She shrugged, regaining her composure, and we started walking again. "Oh, that. They asked if we'd seen anyone along the footpath who didn't belong. I forget how they worded it. It seemed like an odd question. We don't have a lot of traffic. I mean, the path leads to the mobile-home park at one end, and dead-ends at the other."

"You're right. The hard-core joggers aren't interested in that short stretch. But every now and then, I do see someone outside the neighborhood walking by."

"Me too. But never anything—or anyone—out of the ordinary. Anyway, I figured their questions had to do with all that digging."

"Were you home then? While they were searching?"

"Yes, but we couldn't see anything. Do you know what they found? Whatever it was, they whisked it out of sight pretty fast."

"They didn't tell me either. I'm guessing it was a knife—supposedly the one that killed Bianca."

Lydia's eyes widened. "What a strange place to hide it!

"Exactly."

"Sharon, if Miguel didn't kill Bianca, who do you think did?"

Chapter 34

Call it fate. Or maybe an omen. But at that moment, a figure emerged from under one of the umbrellas and strode toward us. As she came closer, I recognized the red wig sprouting from below the large straw hat. Thelma.

She blocked our path and began berating me. "You're such a phony!"

"Guilty as charged."

I'd hoped my comment would derail her, but it bypassed her radar.

Her eyes blazed with fury. "You tried to trick my husband. Playing the dumb blonde, pretending you wanted a new car!"

Her complexion flitted across *my* radar. Was the blotchiness caused by the unflattering yellow of her poncho or by her rage at me?

"I do want a new car."

"No, not just any car. One like...like...."

Like the car your husband provided Bianca?

"Like the Jag?" I asked.

"You tried to set him up!"

I started to move around Thelma, but she stepped closer and grabbed my arm.

I shook her off. "Don't touch me."

Barky, the hair on his neck bristling, gave off a low growl to match mine. Thelma released my arm, but didn't move away. Lydia, saucer-eyed, stood motionless, as if planted in the sand.

"Set him up for what, Thelma?" I asked.

"Quit playing innocent."

I held out my hands, palms upward. "I'm not playing. I'm truly curious. I met with Slim at his Car Emporium. I told him I was interested in a red Jag. He said he didn't have one. End of story." Despite this greatly condensed version of our meeting, I still couldn't imagine how it had affected him in any way.

"You wanted to trick him into confessing. Confessing to something he hadn't done."

Ouch. Not exactly. I had hoped he'd incriminate himself, but that didn't happen.

"*And* you're working hand-in-glove with Lt. Richmond," she added triumphantly.

News to Lt. Richmond. I folded my arms across my chest. "Where did you get that idea?"

Thelma put her hands on her hips and continued to steam. "Isn't it obvious? We all know your nephew is guilty. But have they arrested him? No. You talk to Slim, then to Lt. Richmond, and the next thing we know, the cops are knocking on *our* door."

"Whoa. You're putting together a lot of mish-mash. The truth is, Miguel is innocent. Therefore the police don't have anything to link him to Bianca's murder. Therefore they're questioning lots of people. If Slim isn't guilty, they don't have anything on him either. So what's the problem?"

"You lawyers are all alike. You talk good, but you're tricky."

And you're wacko.

"I guess that says it all, so we'll be on our way." I nudged Lydia, who still seemed to be in a trance.

Without warning, Thelma turned her venom on Lydia. "What about *your* husband? Are they questioning him? A known pedophile?"

I felt myself turn as rigid as Lydia, the blood draining from my face.

Chapter 35

Lydia suddenly sprang to life. In the blink of an eye, she dropped Barky's leash and shoved Thelma backwards with both hands. "How dare you!"

Thelma stumbled, but stayed upright. Barky snarled and flung all four pounds of himself at her with little effect.

"Get your nasty dog off me!"

Lydia looked ready to strike again, fingers curling into fists. I quickly recovered my own momentum, retrieved the leash, and reined in Barky. With the terrier no longer a threat, Thelma lunged toward Lydia. Still holding Barky, I reached out with my free hand, seized Thelma's right hand, and bent her thumb backwards in one swift motion.

She cried out in pain, too stunned to continue her attack. I should amend that. She backed away from us, cradling her injured hand in her left hand, then took up the verbal abuse again. "You're a phony too, Lydia. Pretending to be so lily-white while your pervert husband molests teenagers."

I flung my arm across Lydia before she could retaliate.

"One word of this," I said to Thelma, "and I'll have you up for slander so fast you'll end your days in prison."

"You can't do that."

"Try me. Oh, and I'll throw in 'planting false evidence' and 'obstructing justice' for good measure."

Thelma flushed, the varied hues of her complexion growing more pronounced. "I don't know what you're **talking** about."

"I think you do."

She tossed her head, turned and stalked off. Her thumb was already turning blue and had to be throbbing. I wondered if I'd broken it. She struggled to dismantle the umbrella. Then she gathered it and her beach towel and flounced off.

Lydia was in tears—a mixture of hurt, anger, and frustration. She picked up Barky and held him close. "Sharon, she's lying."

"I figured that. I wasn't exactly truthful either. I *wish* I could do all those things I threatened."

"I know. Some things are impossible to prove. We've already been down the slander path. It's ugly. Everybody suffers, and nobody goes to prison."

"I'm sorry."

"I don't know what got into me. But thanks for defending me. And for not asking questions."

"It must be hard to talk about."

"I need to sit down for a few minutes." She took a few steps closer to the dunes, then sank down on the sand. She brought her knees up to her chest, wrapped her arms around her legs, and rested her curly head on her knees. Barky's leash hung loosely around her wrist, while Barky leaned against her and whimpered softly.

"I'm a little shaky myself," I said, sitting next to her and putting my arm around her shoulders.

We stayed there quietly for a few minutes.

"We'd better go before our sunscreen starts to give out," Lydia said, straightening up and pulling her visor forward.

We stood and brushed the sand off our jeans, then resumed our walk home.

Lydia looked out at the gulf, then at me. "She was right that Tom and I are phonies."

173

"Oh?"

"Tom did his stint in the Navy, but he certainly didn't retire. He was a bookkeeper. We were both active in our church, and he began to feel he was called to the ministry. I was in total agreement. Right after seminary, he was assigned to a congregation in a small midwestern town. He was very well liked."

She spoke in a monotone, and I wondered how many times she'd recited this in her mind.

"We were there four years, then went to a church where they needed a youth pastor. That went well for about a year. And then—"

I waited.

An edge came to her voice. "Then there was this young girl—sixteen. Tom calls her 'troubled.' I have another word for it. You can probably see what's coming."

"I'm guessing she made false accusations."

"'Improper advances.' Most people believed in Tom. But a few were already up in arms about sex scandals, and too willing to take her side. He got his picture in the paper, of course. When he was cleared, there was a little note of apology somewhere.

"He stayed on for another year, but felt like he was under a microscope. We did come down here on vacation for a number of years—that part's true. Early on, a mutual friend introduced us to Roque. Turned out to be a godsend! We grew to be good friends, and—that awful summer when we showed up so distraught, Roque knew right away something was wrong. When Tom finally confided in Roque, he was outraged. He encouraged us to move here permanently, get a fresh start."

"That sounds like Tío Roque.... How did Thelma find out?"

"Probably from the Internet. That's how Bianca found out."

"Bianca!"

"Oh, yes. I suspect Bianca looked up everyone on the Internet. She discovered that Doris used to be a stripper."

"Really? Doris?"

"Apparently so. Bianca asked Doris for some hush money—this was several months ago—but Doris decided to tell everyone herself. Made a joke out of it—you know Doris. She said she was not only young and stupid once, but also a looker, and that's what she wanted folks to remember."

I had to chuckle. "Good for her. Did all this come out at Mayra's?"

"Oh, heavens, no. Well, the 'confession' did. But Bianca never came over for coffee. No, she was much more sneaky about approaching people. I suppose. Sneaky about approaching Tom, anyway. He volunteers at a senior citizen center, and she cornered him there."

"And if Bianca could find out so easily...."

"The cops did come by to check us out. I guess they were satisfied, because we haven't heard from them again. Even so, it was a little nerve-wracking. I keep thinking, *Won't this ever go away?*"

I was having a hard time processing all this. I found myself wondering "which Lydia" was real. I wanted to believe her. She seemed so honest—but then she always had. Lydia, with her warm brown eyes, had always been so kind and gentle. Lashing out at Thelma seemed totally out of character. Then again, what did I know?

Chapter 36

Ryan had finished weeding and was enjoying a Tecate on the patio when I came through the back gate. I walked toward him mechanically, my bravado depleted. He set the beer on the cabana table and rose from the wicker chair. "What happened to you?"

"I need a hug and a cup of yerba buena, in that order."

Ryan held me for a few minutes without speaking, simply stroking my hair, which was probably standing on end. His arm still around me, we walked into the kitchen. I sat at the table while he boiled water and didn't mention that the day was a little warm for hot tea. After he set my brew before me, I added sugar, the warmth and the sweetness as soothing as the tea itself. He retrieved his own cold drink, then sat across from me.

"What can you tell me about Tom?" I asked at last.

Ryan looked surprised. "What do you want to know?"

"You said you liked him, so I just wondered...."

"Well, I didn't spend that much time with him, but he seemed friendly enough. Straightforward. Knowledgeable. Let's see...what else? He does a lot of volunteering. We're both history buffs.... Why?"

The pieces came tumbling out, as disconnected as a kaleidoscope gone amok: Thelma's accusations (plural), Lydia's reaction, my own attack on Thelma, Lydia's disturbing revelations, Bianca's methods of digging up dirt—even Doris's supposed past.

"Lydia never did tell me how they handled Bianca's threats. After seeing the way Lydia went after Thelma, well—"

"Maybe she figured the gossip died with Bianca. Must have given her a jolt to realize it was more widespread."

A wave of nausea swept over me, despite the healing effects of the tea. *What if the gossip's true?* Another thought intruded almost simultaneously. *Do people wonder the same about Miguel?*

* * *

Ryan and I were quiet on the drive back to San Antonio. I couldn't decide if the weekend had been too long or too short. So much had happened, and so little had been accomplished. I felt frustrated, knowing that the more time went by, the less chance we had of solving Bianca's murder.

Working in conjunction with the Port Aransas Police, the San Antonio cops had questioned Miguel again. I suppose they were stymied too, since they hadn't arrested him—or anyone else.

Monday morning after firing up the computer in my office, I debated with myself about checking out Lydia's story. I was sure Tío Roque would never have invited them down if he'd had any doubts. Still, it was something I needed to see for myself.

The search engine showed lots of "Tom (and Thomas) Wilsons," but not too many "Rev. Thomas Wilsons." I finally found the right one. The most recent news story—brief, as Lydia had said—verified that the "alleged incident" had been scrapped. The underage "victim" proved to be an attention-seeking liar (though the paper hadn't worded it that way). Her name wasn't listed, of course. No reason to sully *her* reputation. Disgusted, I didn't search further.

* * *

Nearly three weeks went by. During the day, I immersed myself in work. But at night I had a recurring dream about looking up Thelma and Slim on the Internet. I kept getting error messages on the computer—always some version of "You're looking in the wrong place."

"Well, where am I supposed to look?" I finally yelled in frustration, waking up both Ryan and myself.

"Wha—? Look for what?" Ryan mumbled.

"I wish I knew."

*   *   *

Tío Roque invited the whole family—rather, our little segment of it—to spend Thanksgiving with him on Mustang Island. Miguel was hesitant, but we persuaded him this would be a good time to replace bad memories with good ones.

Our prediction turned out to be true. Since Tío's place was small, we gathered at the Meléndez cottage, with everyone pitching in to prepare the meal. The familiar aromas of turkey, dressing, and candied yams flooded us, and we spent the afternoon laughing, reminiscing, and overeating.

I had hoped Mayra would join us, but she was spending the day with her godson in Rockport. When I called to wish her happy Thanksgiving, she told me she was looking forward to seeing me over coffee the next morning.

"I don't think that's such a good idea," Ryan said, when I mentioned it on the way back from dinner.

"Why?"

"There's something I probably should have told you before, but I've been putting it off."

My heart did a flip-flop. "What is it?"

We reached our cottage, came in and sat on the beachwood chairs in the living room.

"Didn't you ever wonder why Mayra's taken such an interest in the murder?" Ryan asked.

"I think the whole town is curious."

"But Mayra's in the middle of it all. Right from the start. She called you—what—a minute and a half after the cops first questioned us."

The Hardy boys. Sgts. Fay and Bullis.

"She keeps track of everyone through you, through Gloria Bullis, through Thelma—probably her best source—"

"C'mon, Ryan. Okay, Mayra's a little gossipy, but she's not malicious."

Ryan's jaw set, but his eyes showed sadness rather than anger. "At one time the gossip was *about* her. I wasn't sure whether to believe it, gossip being what it is. But the more I thought about it, the more it added up."

I had a childish urge to put my hands over my ears. Instead I folded them in my lap and willed myself to sit still.

"Remember when I had lunch with Roger?" Ryan said. "Somehow her name came up—I think I'd mentioned the luau. Anyway, he used to live in Port Aransas, and he told me that Mayra's husband was in a boating accident about ten years ago. Supposedly an accident. Mayra was with him at the time. The day was calm and all that. No apparent reason for the guy to go overboard, much less drown."

Ryan took a breath. I was still too nonplussed to say anything.

"There was a lot of talk. Obviously, she lived it down. And it was a long time ago. But maybe Bianca found something incriminating—something she could blackmail Mayra with."

"After all this time?"

"Bianca was pretty conniving. Smarter than I think we gave her credit for."

"I just can't picture Mayra—stabbing Bianca."

"If she really did get rid of her husband, I'm sure she'd have no compunction about getting rid of Bianca."

"You're forgetting something. If there was gossip, Tío Roque must have heard it too. He wouldn't have gotten involved with her."

"You and Tío have this blind spot when it comes to loyalty."

"And sometimes we're right," I said stubbornly.

"And sometimes you're wrong. Sharon, be careful."

Chapter 37

I caught up with Lydia on my way to Mayra's the next morning. A sense of déjà vu overtook me. Here we were taking the same old companionable walks we'd taken before.

"It's good to be going to coffee together," Lydia said, reading my mind. "After our run-in with Thelma at the beach, I almost quit going. But I had a long talk with myself, and I'm stronger now."

The feeling of déjà vu increased when we joined the gathering around Mayra's kitchen table: A heightened awareness of the coziness I'd often taken for granted.

Here were women I'd come to like, future friends, I hoped: Doris, brash and funny; Gloria, sassy and sympathetic. Here were those I'd already come to consider friends: Fina and Lydia, warm and generous.

And Mayra. Mayra in another of her flowing muumuus— one with large swirls of purple and silver this time—and with the ubiquitous chopsticks in her swept-up black hair. Tears stung my eyes, and I focused on the coffee in front of me. Mayra and I had established a bond I still couldn't shake off. But I knew nothing would be the same after today.

Conversation hummed around and over me. I could distinguish voices, but not words. Not until Lydia spoke up.

"I've been giving this a lot of thought," she said, "and I want to clear the air."

Everyone stopped chattering and looked at Lydia expectantly.

"Some rumors have surfaced...." She looked directly at Thelma. "Tom is an ordained minister. Some false accusations were made against him in the small town where we lived. Most people supported him, and we stayed for a long while. But we eventually decided the best way to put it all behind us was to move. No, we weren't *forced* to move. And we didn't change our names. However, it isn't something we like to think about, much less dwell on." She paused. "But then the gossip started."

A couple of women looked uncomfortable. Most simply looked puzzled.

"Lydia," Fina said, "the Tom I know is a blessing to our whole community. He brightens up the Assisted Living home whenever he visits. And what would the food pantry at the Methodist Church do without him?"

"Amen," said Doris. "It's a good thing I never heard otherwise, or I would've had to beat up someone."

Doris gave Thelma a long look, and I wondered if her poison had already reached Doris's ears, despite her words.

I wished I could bring up what was troubling me and it could be resolved so simply, but I knew I'd have to face Mayra in private.

Chapter 38

"What's on your mind, Sharon?" Mayra asked after everyone else had left and we were sitting alone in her kitchen.

"Gossip. Rumors. Miguel.... You."

"I see." She got up, fetched the coffeepot, poured us each another cup, and sat at the table again. "I suppose those things are all tied together somehow?"

I sighed. "I don't know. I've actually been trying to untie them."

We were both silent, while I stirred creamer into my coffee and kept stirring longer than necessary.

"Tell me about your husband, Mayra. About his death."

"Well, that's a little blunt." Her eyes narrowed, and I couldn't read her expression.

I put my spoon down and looked at her. "Yes it is. I feel like I'm running out of time. And I'm also tired of going down blind alleys."

"I can assure you, this is another blind alley."

"Was Bianca blackmailing you?"

"Is that what you think?"

"I know she searched the Internet for anything and everything she could find to hurt people."

Mayra studied me a moment. "She did approach me. Just like you, she came straight to the point. I wanted to laugh in her face. At the same time—you're right—it hurt."

Stay tough. Stay tough. "I'm sorry. I truly am." *So much for tough.*

Her face softened. "Your reasons are different though. She wanted power, and she enjoyed tormenting people. You—you just don't know whether to trust me or not. Am I right?"

"Yes."

"But you're not afraid of me."

"I guess not. I'm here."

"Oh, Sharon. Well, for the record, here's what happened. We took our little sailboat out in the bay. Felipe—my husband—was fishing, and I was just relaxing, imagining pictures in the clouds. All of a sudden, he leaned over too far, which wasn't like him, and the next thing I knew, he was in the water. His face was white, contorted.

"We both knew how to swim, and besides, we were wearing life vests, but he wasn't making any move to get back on the boat. I jumped in and grabbed his hand, pulling him to the edge. But I couldn't lift him. I started yelling, but it was a while before someone rescued us. Rather, got us back to shore."

"I thought—I heard—he drowned. It sounds like he had a heart attack."

"He did. And the autopsy proved it. If anyone bothered to read the report."

"Then why do you think the rumors started?"

Mayra raised an eyebrow. "For one thing, because my husband was a good sailor, a good swimmer, it looked—odd. I think the real reason was envy. Jealousy. Whatever you want to call it. We were very well off financially. And I became a 'rich widow.'"

"And we—Bianca and I both—brought back painful memories."

"It's surprising the pain is still so sharp after all these years."

184

The tears began rolling down my cheeks.

Mayra reached over and patted my hand, then handed me a Kleenex. "It cuts, but it doesn't linger. Don't blame yourself. You're just protecting Miguel."

I wiped my eyes and composed myself.

"I think," I said softly, "you're protecting someone too. Which is really what I need to know."

"How much longer can this go on?" Mayra murmured. She looked beyond me without focusing on anything.

"I thought you were going to help me clear Miguel."

"I intended to. But that was before...." She looked at me again. "Don't worry. If they haven't arrested him by now, they won't."

"So he'll just live with rumors and suspicion the rest of his life. I don't think you'd wish that on anyone."

She stood and cleared away the coffee cups. "Talk to John."

Chapter 39

"I'll let myself out," I told Mayra's back.

As I reached the door, she called out after me, "Wait, I'll go with you."

I hadn't planned to see John right away. I needed time to think. Still, I welcomed Mayra's offer.

"He should be home now," she said. "He hasn't found anyone to replace Bianca in the office, so he usually closes down for an hour at lunchtime."

"Your suggestion came out of the blue. I don't know what to say to him."

"I didn't think you had a problem being blunt."

Ouch. "You haven't forgiven me, have you."

"It's not that. It's just hard choosing between friends."

For the second time since I'd known her, Mayra seemed to age before my eyes. Her shoulders drooped, bearing the weight of the choice she was making.

We walked past Mr. Edwards' house, past the house that used to be Bianca's (still unoccupied), and over to John's. He didn't answer Mayra's knock, so she cracked the door open and peeked in.

"John? John? Are you home?"

No answer. She opened the door wider. "That's strange. The television's on."

"Maybe he's in the bathroom."

"Maybe."

We waited another few minutes, and Mayra called again.

"Go away." His voice was muffled, and I couldn't follow the sound.

"He must be in the den. Hurry!" Mayra said, her alarm overcoming her previous reluctance.

We opened the door to the extra bedroom that John had converted into a den. The faint smell of alcohol floated out to us. John, looking gray and beaten-down, but still dressed in suit and tie, slouched in a straight chair facing the door. His arms hung by his side, and in his left hand was an army knife.

"John, what are you doing?" Mayra asked briskly, as if she was asking about something as commonplace as fixing the sink.

He frowned. "I'm thinking."

"What about?"

"About?" The question seemed to puzzle him. "I'm tired of thinking."

"Good. I'll make some coffee. Sharon, can you find your way around the kitchen? You make the coffee, and I'll keep John company."

"I don't want company," he mumbled.

"Nonsense."

I went to the kitchen, set my purse on the counter, and located the coffeepot. How did this one work? Which canister held the coffee? Where were the filters? How many scoops? Why were my hands shaking? Why was I stressing over this?

Sharon, think.

I closed my eyes and took several deep breaths. My cell-phone was in my purse. I should call Ryan. Or maybe Lt. Richmond. Then another idea came to me. Half an idea. I wanted to squeeze a confession out of John before anyone else showed up. I only hoped he wouldn't harm himself—or us—in the meantime.

I got the coffee made, but didn't think I could manage a single swallow. I poured cups for John and Mayra and carried them back to the den, my purse over my shoulder.

Nothing had changed. Mayra was still talking in a matter-of-fact voice, and John was still staring ahead like a zombie. She coaxed him into sampling his coffee, but he banged the cup down on the desk next to him after a few gulps. He still hadn't loosened his grip on the knife.

"Now John, it's not your fault Bertha died," Mayra said.

I gave a start, but she'd shifted gears so smoothly, he didn't even blink.

I sat down in a chair facing him. Mayra was sitting at right angles to both of us. I placed my purse on the end table beside me and eased out my cell phone.

"It was more my fault," Mayra was saying. "I shouldn't have told you about her threatening me."

"Not your fault. She harassed other people too. I told her to quit. Not that it did any good."

He sounded almost coherent. Either he hadn't drunk that much booze, or the coffee was kicking in, or both.

"John, you've put up with so much," I said. "What happened?"

He squinted in my direction, then looked at the ceiling. Mayra gave me a warning look.

"She was crazy," he said. "I went crazy too."

"You were sick," Mayra said. "She had no right to come over and blame you."

Blame him for what? What was going on here?

"She was crazy," he repeated. "I still don't know what she was talking about."

I quietly opened my cell phone, set it to "video," and slid it onto the end table, all the while praying that I'd aimed it in the right direction and that my batteries wouldn't run out.

"She wasn't making sense?" I prompted.

"She comes over in the middle of the night," John said, as if the scene were replaying itself before his eyes. "Gets me out of bed to yell at me. Accuses me of telling her boyfriend things that made him dump her. I never said a word to him!"

John punctuated his agitation by stabbing the air with his knife. I was partly alarmed and partly relieved. At least his anger was directed at Bertha/Bianca instead of himself.

"I keep waiting for her to wind down, so I can take something for my headache and go back to bed. I go to the kitchen for some pain pills, and she follows me. And then she carries on about how I've ruined her life, and she can't live without Miguel."

Mayra and I sat spellbound, neither of us wanting to stop the tide. I wondered how much Mayra already knew.

"So without any warning, Bertha pulls out the drawer where I keep my army knife. She says she's going to kill herself, and she makes a couple of slashes in her stomach. Not deep. It has to have hurt, but she's determined to slice again."

John's thoughts seemed to turn further inward. "Something comes over me. I grab her by the hair, take the knife away from her—" He reached out and clenched his right fist while pointing the knife downward with his left hand, his actions in sync with his words.

"And I say—I say—" John's weapon clattered to the floor and he covered his face with both hands. When he took his hands away, his face was wet with tears. "I can't believe I yelled at her like that," he said softly. "I said, 'you can't even do this right,' and then I stabbed her."

I shut off the phone. I had my confession, but I felt no sense of joy.

Chapter 40

There was more, of course. In his feverish state, John blamed Miguel for Bianca's misery. John wrapped Bianca in a plastic tarp, bundled her body into the Jag and drove over to the cottage he thought was occupied by Miguel. John then rolled her body onto the edge of the lawn, not risking alerting anyone by carrying her closer to the cottage. Only Barky knew something was wrong.

After parking the Jag back in Bianca's carport, he'd gone home and scrubbed away the blood on the tile floor, knowing it would never pass a forensics test, but hoping it would never come to that. He stuffed the tarp behind some tools in his shed till he could throw it into the dumpster a few weeks later.

My video-phone had captured John's left side (the side with the army knife) and some bookcases. The words were muffled in places, but clear where it counted. John confessed to the police later, so my record was only a backup anyway.

Mayra put the kaffee klatch on hold for a week or two, then realized the solidarity of friends was healing. I hear Thelma still shows up occasionally. I won't say she's turned over a new leaf, but apparently she's less vocal.

Mayra's attempts to help me had been sincere all along. I felt bad about doubting her, but she said I'd done her a favor in the long run. My openness—and Lydia's—had made her aware that some misunderstandings, as well as some serious problems, had been hidden too long. Ornella Hewett came to mind. We agreed that it was time to quit pretending not to notice her addiction. We wanted her and Keith both to know that friends would rally around them throughout her road to recovery.

Mayra had never suspected John until he confided in her several days after Bianca's death, saying it was all a terrible accident. In a way, this was true. Bianca's self-inflicted "wounds" turned out to be fairly superficial after all. With her penchant for drama, it seems likely her purpose was simply to play on John's presumed guilt for supposedly having betrayed her past to Miguel. (Of course, neither she nor John ever knew it was actually Leo who had told Miguel about her lies.)

John had turned the knife on her purely on impulse. Afterwards, he promised Mayra he'd go to the police, and she kept waiting for him to follow through.

Efforts are being made to see that John ends up in a psychiatric facility rather than prison. Tío Roque has felt for some time that John has been struggling with PTSD while trying to hide it. Even as a lawyer, I can't outguess the legal system, but I'd rather see John helped than punished.

One question that will remain unanswered has to do with Bianca's photo album. My guess is that Cordelia found it on her earlier visit and felt entitled to keep it since "her" Ernie's pictures were in it. Rather than admit she'd stolen it, she made up one lie after another, which turned out to have no bearing on Bianca's murder anyway.

So what's ahead? With cooler weather, our trips to the Island will be fewer. Ryan thinks we should spend Christmas where it's *really* cold. Last summer we drove through Las Vegas, New Mexico, but didn't take time to explore the town. It sounds more and more inviting. A quiet holiday by the fire in front of the Christmas tree; drinking cider and singing carols while the snow swirls merrily outside—as picturesque as a greeting card. Oh, did I mention? The hotel where we'd like to stay has a ghost. Yes, a quiet Christmas indeed.